Antonia's lips were entirely too near for reasonableness. He kissed them. And met a response so intense that it took his breath away and destroyed the last vestiges of his common sense.

After their first start of surprise her widened eyes had closed, her fingers had sent his hat toppling to entangle with his hair, and she had simply surrendered to the wonderful, heady glow that overpowered her. She would never have dreamed that the mere touch of his lips, the teasing of tongues, could turn the balance of nature topsy-turvy. All she really knew was that she wanted the moment to last forever—and this man to love her.

Both notions were ridiculous, of course. . . .

SCANDAL BROTH

Marian Devon

FAWCETT CREST • NEW YORK

A Fawcett Crest Book
Published by Ballantine Books
Copyright © 1987 by Marian Pope Rettke

Library of Congress Catalog Card Number: 86-91827

ISBN 0-449-21039-1

Manufactured in the United States of America

First Edition: June 1987

Chapter One

The quill scratched rapidly, faltered, stopped. Miss Antonia Thorpe brushed her nose absently with the goose feather and eyed her composition, quite unaware that she herself was under surveillance. "March 5, 1815," she read.

Dear Papa,
  I arrived yesterday. Your concern was wasted. I proved an excellent sailor, not queasy once. Had the channel been rough, however, the story might have been quite different.

Oh, dear. Enough of that. Papa wouldn't be pleased to pay for an extra sheet, and he hated trying to read a crossed letter. She must bring him quickly up-to-date. Antonia sighed, dipped her pen in the inkwell, and tried again.

  The Hall is even more grand than you described it. And everyone has been

Once more the quill's scratching ceased. This time the young composer tried blowing upon the feather for inspiration. None came. And she could not possibly write what was foremost in her mind —that she didn't like Uncle Edwin above half, found her Cousin Rosamond insipid, and England too bleak for words.

1

The pen made another journey to the inkwell, then hovered indecisively above the paper. "Oh, botheration!" Antonia glared indignantly at the spreading inkblot.

"It seems I'm interrupting you, Miss Thorpe."

The voice that jerked her head up was deep, aristocratic, and tinged with irony. A gentleman wearing creamy buckskins and a superbly cut dark blue riding coat was standing in the open doorway watching her. "Of course, if my timing is inconvenient," he continued, managing to sound gentlemanly and faintly sarcastic at the same time, "we can always cancel this interview."

His actions, however, belied such flexibility. For the young man stepped inside, closing the door behind him. As he crossed the room to loom over her writing table, Antonia grew faintly alarmed. She looked up at him warily, feeling more at sea than at any moment during her recent voyage. What she saw was a man of twenty-eight who looked slightly older, who was rather above the average height and well above the average handsome. But most of all, and for reasons of his own, he was also above the average hostile.

Antonia; not normally so easy to intimidate, swallowed hard before inquiring, "You wished to speak to me, sir?" Her voice sounded tremulous to her own ears.

The gentleman abandoned any desire he might still have had to bridle his disgust. "Frankly, Miss Thorpe, I find your excessive missishness a bore. Keeping me dangling in the doorway with your faked preoccupation was too coy by half. We both know why I'm here. So under the circumstances it seems ludicrous to indulge in these charades. Ours is a business arrangement, purely and simply, and to view it otherwise is a hypocrisy I, for one, find intolerable."

"I can assure you, sir, that indulging in charades is the furthest thing from my mind." Antonia tried to make her tone placating while she glanced furtively around the room for a handy weapon. But the library did not lend itself to self-defense. What a pity her uncle had no taste for weaponry. True, there were some weighty tomes upon the shelves that lined the paneled walls, but getting to them could pose a problem. The brass poker by the Adam fireplace looked substantial enough to be effective but was also too far removed for practicality. The inkwell seemed less adequate but was at hand.

The deranged gentleman, Antonia concluded, was made more dangerous by lacking the physical prerequisites for a bedlamite. The deep blue eyes showed no tendency to roll; his gaze, in fact, threatened to impale her to her chair. Not only did his raven hair lack the required wisps of straw, it also was meticulously arranged, à la Titus, or she missed her guess. A square-cut jaw and high cheekbones were bound to give a deceptive look of character even to a maniac, she supposed. But despite all appearances to the contrary, there could be no doubt about it, the man confronting her was stark-raving mad. Her only resource was to humor him till she could summon help. She felt her way carefully.

"You spoke of a business arrangement we should discuss. I fear the matter has slipped my mind. Momentarily. But if you'll refresh my memory, I'm sure we can arrive at an understanding." To further demonstrate her desire to please, Antonia stretched the muscles of her face in a manner calculated to produce a smile. The effort evidently went awry. At least it failed to elicit the appropriate response. For instead of beaming back, the gentleman's countenance grew even more thunderous.

"See here, Miss Thorpe. I only arrived home yesterday. And"—he looked pointedly at the ormolu clock on the mantelpiece—"I have a great deal to do before leaving for London in the morning. I was given to understand that everything had been arranged by our respective parents and all I had to do was put in an appearance here. Now, if this directness doesn't coincide with your romantic notions, well then, I'm sorry. But I'm damned if I'm going down on one

3

knee to you. Let's at least begin our liaison with honesty, if nothing else.''

His blue eyes had narrowed during this impassioned speech. Antonia's had grown saucer-sized. She had ceased to be concerned about his mental state; it was her own that now concerned her. Surely she was imagining this whole scene. ''Are you *offering* for me, sir?'' she choked.

He swore. Not quite underneath his breath, if indeed that had ever been his intent. ''Miss Thorpe, you might as well know now that I am not a patient man. Just why you've chosen to be so coy about all this escapes me, but I'd be much obliged if you'd drop the pose. My father informs me that every detail—including your compliance, I might add—has been worked out between your father and himself. Furthermore, since you do stand to profit more from the arrangement than I do, though it's hardly gallant of me to say so, it does seem the outside of enough for me to be expected to jump through hoops. Frankly, Miss Thorpe, despite all my celebrated failings, it seems to me that you are to be congratulated on this match. Young ladies of your dubious background do not often get the opportunity to become baronesses.''

''Are you calling me a cit, sir?'' Antonia might be confused on every other point, but she did know an insult when she heard it. Her apprehension was rapidly turning into anger, overriding all her instinct regarding the proper kid-glove handling of bedlamites. She rose to her feet and glared across the table. ''I don't know who you think you are, sir, to cast aspersions on my background. What's more, I don't believe for one moment that my father would arrange my marriage without consulting me. My father simply could not—'' She suddenly faltered while her righteous indignation sputtered and went out. She stared up at the stranger, suddenly appalled. ''At least I don't th-think he would,'' she stammered. ''Of course, I didn't really see why he insisted that I come here. In fact, I'll grant you

4

that it made very little sense to me at the time. But I never dreamed . . . Oh, how could he!" She sank down into her seat. "Of all the shabby, despicable—"

"Well, I may owe you an apology, Miss Thorpe," the gentleman said grudgingly. "Unless you're a better actress than Mrs. Siddons, it seems you really didn't know our marriage has been arranged. I agree that your father's conduct leaves a lot to be desired, but let's not allow that fact to divert us from the purpose of this meeting. For even if my offer does catch you unawares, I can't believe that you seriously object to it."

Antonia, who had been running through her father's professed reasons for packing her off to England—reasons that had seemed lame at the time and now appeared devious—returned her full attention to her arrogant intended. "If you can't believe that I seriously object to marrying you, well, then, sir, I can only say that you show a serious want of imagination."

"I beg your pardon?"

"Am I not plain enough? I don't care what sort of arrangements my father may have made behind my back, I wouldn't marry you if you were the last—" She snapped her teeth shut on the cliché. The situation called for something fresh and new. But it was not forthcoming.

"Are you refusing me, Miss Thorpe?" His lip curled in disbelief.

"How could I possibly be? You haven't actually offered for me, have you?"

"So, we're back to that again." His jaw tightened. "Very well, then. If you must make me perform, so be it. Only I won't go down on one knee, by God. Well, this is it. Pray pay attention. Miss Thorpe"—his voice was as insulting as the exaggerated gesture with which he placed a hand upon his heart— "will you do me the honor of becoming my wife?"

"No."

"No?" His eyebrows rose. "Don't play games, Miss Thorpe. My father only requires that I ask, you know."

"Well, you just did so. Now please leave."

Relief warred with disbelief upon his face. "I trust you don't intend to change your mind the moment I walk out of here. For, let me warn you, I shall consider this your final word."

"Well, not quite my *final* word." Antonia surprised herself by discovering a need to prolong his agony. She had found it rather galling to have her answer taken in the spirit of a gallows reprieve. So now she gleefully watched the hope fade from his eyes and the hauteur return.

"So, it is not your final word?"

"Oh, dear me, no. My final word is that I find your attitude insulting and your arrogance insufferable. And I can feel nothing but deep pity for the poor female who does agree to be your baroness. For I would not marry you, sir," she finished triumphantly, "if you were next in line for king!"

The speech, intended to be crushing, fell far wide of the mark. For the gentleman gave her a bow that was only halfway mocking and flashed a smile that came close to taking her breath away. "Well, then, Miss Thorpe, may I say that you have my admiration—to say nothing of my gratitude. For I never expected you to have the courage to defy your father. Nor did he, I'll wager!

"Well, now, pray forgive me for wasting so much of your time. And, if I'm not being premature again, allow me to wish you and your curate happy. Good day, Miss Thorpe." His step was light as he crossed the room and shut the library door with a firm click of the latch behind him.

Antonia sat rooted in her chair and stared at the closed door. "My curate?" she whispered faintly. "Wish me happy with a *curate*? Dear heavens, I was right in the first place. The poor gentleman is raving mad!"

Miss Thorpe did not long remain the only person to harbor misgivings about the Honorable Fitzhugh Denholm's mental stability. Her uncle, Sir Edwin Thorpe, who had been lurking in an antechamber off the hall in order to be the first to congratulate his distinguished visitor and welcome him into the family, could only gape incredulously after Mr. Denholm's terse announcement. "B-but that's impossible!" he blurted. "She can't have refused your offer. She wouldn't! Oh, you must be mistaken."

"I assure you, sir, that I am not." Mr. Denholm made very little effort to hide his distaste for the rotund, encroaching little man gaping up at him. "Miss Thorpe refused me in no uncertain terms."

He was thwarted in his attempt to walk on past Sir Edwin by that gentleman's convulsive clutch upon his sleeve. "Oh, well, now. You mustn't refine too much on that, sir. Why, it don't mean a thing." Sir Edwin tried without much success for jocularity. "A man of the world like yourself must know what women are."

"I'm man of the world enough to realize that no member of my sex knows what women are." He shook off the restraining hand. "Now, if you'll excuse me."

"Why, the chit just don't wish to appear overanxious, that's all." Sir Edwin interposed himself between the exit and his guest. "The ladies like to be coaxed, don't you know. Why, it's practically a rule with 'em not to accept a gentleman's first offer. Ain't considered good ton. Oh, but she means to have you, all right. You'll see."

"That I will not." Sir Edwin recoiled under the icy stare. "I have complied with my father's wishes and offered for Miss Thorpe. She in her turn has refused me. The matter is at an end."

A powdered footman, struggling to keep his face impassive, leaped for the door. But, as he afterward related in the servants' hall, "His nibs almost beat me to it and opened it himself—he was that anxious to be gone! Couldn't wait to see the last of Sir Edwin or I'm a Frenchy! And may God strike me blind if this ain't the very gospel, just before I went to shut the door behind him, I heard that starchy gentry cove go off whistling. Merry as a gig he was."

Chapter Two

"Rosamond!"

Regardless of whatever damage his nervous system might have been suffering, Sir Edwin had found tongue. His bellow preceded him down the hall and reverberated within the library where Antonia was trying to resume her composition. "So, there you are!" he thundered from the doorway as she raised her head. "Oh, blast it, no. It's you!"

Is there something about that threshold that turns English gentlemen into instant boors? Antonia wondered as she struggled not to take offense. And once again she was struck by the evenhanded treatment fate had accorded to two brothers. Her father had got the looks and charm; her uncle the estate and the business acumen. The only thing the two Thorpes had in common was that both had married delicate females who'd died young. Sir Edwin now looked ready to follow suit from a fit of apoplexy. "Is something wrong, Uncle?" she inquired with sympathy.

"Wrong? Wrong! I should say something's wrong!" Sir Edwin swelled with indignation while his niece watched in alarm, expecting his waistcoat buttons to become projectiles at any moment. "Things are as wrong as they possibly can be, miss. I would never have believed that my own flesh and blood could make a mockery of all me dreams. Rosamond!" he shouted again. "Where is that girl?"

Antonia glanced upward at the crystal chandelier, fearful

the glass had cracked. "I rather think Rosamond's gone for a walk, sir. At least, as I was coming downstairs to write Papa, I saw her leave her room wearing a cloak and pattens."

"Going outside! Going for a walk! Running away from home, most likely! Afraid to face me, b'gad, and well she should be. Of all the wretched, ungrateful girls! To fling away her chances with no concern for what it might do to her father! Oh, my God!" Suddenly in need of support, Sir Edwin clutched the edge of the writing table and stared down at his niece. His mouth was working soundlessly, like a beached cod's.

Antonia, on her part, resolved never to sit in that particular spot again. One more encounter like the two endured this morning and she'd swim back to Belgium. Her uncle, after several swallows and a huge gulp of air, managed to croak, "Just how long have you been sitting here?"

"Since about ten-thirty."

"And Rosamond went outdoors, you say, just as you were coming down the stairs?"

"Yes, sir, so I assume."

Sir Edwin just did manage to totter to the nearest wing chair before collapsing. "Then, it was you he talked to." His voice had sunk to whisper level, and his eyes were glazed.

Should she ring for the butler? Antonia wondered. Her uncle appeared to need a restorative, at the very least. But just as she half rose, intending to walk to the bellpull, the scales dropped from her uncle's eyes and he glared at her through a red haze of fury. "Is that what happened, miss?" he spit.

This sudden alteration of mood wiped the bellpull from her mind. Her uncle's latest start demanded full attention. By some freak of nature, had the entire male population of Kent gone queer in the attic this morning? "Is what what happened, sir?" she asked aloud, groping for reality.

"Did the Honorable Fitzhugh Denholm come in here

while you were sitting there?'' A trembling finger pointed accusingly.

"Well, someone certainly did come in. But he hadn't the civility to introduce himself. Now that I think on it, he did say he'd be a baron someday, so I suppose that could make him an Honorable now. I never could keep track of—''

"Will you stop blathering!'' Sir Edwin was on his feet again, his mien choleric. "Just tell me what Mr. Denholm said!''

"Well, I'll try. But it won't be easy. He took me entirely by surprise. And was quite incoherent.''

"Damn it, girl! What exactly did he say?''

"I'm doing my best to remember.'' Antonia had had a tiring morning. Respect for her elders was wearing thin. She glared back at her uncle in kind. "It's not easy to reconstruct the interview, for the gentleman was obviously raving mad—or next door to it. He actually seemed to be offering for me. Said his father and mine had worked the whole thing out—which I'll not believe Papa would do without first telling me. Besides, the gentleman was absolutely furious at the notion. Nasty and insulting. Obviously a bedlamite. For, if that was his idea of a proper marriage offer, I'd hate to be around when he challenged someone to a duel. Still, under normal quarrelsome circumstances perhaps he'd be the soul of amiability.''

"You nincompoop!'' Sir Edwin regained his roar. "Do you realize what you've done? Oh, don't bother looking at me with those big innocent eyes—of course you do! Oh, I knew I never should have agreed to let Adrian foist you off onto me. Bad blood! That's what I told him when he married, and by gad, I've been proved right. Bad blood! Will show up in the third generation every time. A viper in my bosom. That's what your father's sent me—a viper!''

"Uncle Edwin!'' Antonia's voice shook with rage. "How dare you speak to me in such a fashion? There's nothing at all the matter with my blood. Not unless I've inherited some taint from you that I don't know of. For

11

you must be dicked in the nob, sir, to fly up into the boughs this way. Will you please calm down and try to tell me sensibly just what it is you think I've done?''

''Done? Done?'' To match another sudden mood swing, Sir Edwin's voice rang hollow. ''You know perfectly well, young woman, what you've done. And if this is your warped idea of a prank—well, all I can say is that your father at his worst, which was certainly bad enough for a more feckless fellow—'' He pulled himself up short. ''Your father at his worst would not have stooped so low. Bad blood—''

''Uncle Edwin, don't you dare start up about my blood again. Just tell me, calmly, what this is all about. *What am I supposed to have done*?''

''You've pretended to be Rosamond; that's what you've done. You've pretended to be me gel and ruined her life.''

''I've done no such thing. Of all the sap-skulled notions. Why ever would I? Oh, my goodness—'' Stunned disbelief overrode her anger. ''Surely you don't mean—'' A gurgle of laughter inadvertently escaped before her good sense could act as censor. ''Are you trying to say that that odious man actually thought he was offering for Rosamond? Oh, but that's too absurd.''

''Absurd, you say. What's absurd is to pretend you didn't know it. You—you—viper!''

''Uncle, you are making it most difficult for me to maintain my composure. Of course I didn't know it. In the first place, I thought the man was mad. And in the second, he called me 'Miss Thorpe,' which is my name. Even you must admit I've as much right to it as Rosamond. More perhaps. I've had it four months longer. And I certainly never dreamed that a man would offer a serious proposal of marriage to a woman he doesn't even know. Can't recognize. Who *would* think it?''

''Of course he knows her,'' Sir Edwin blustered. ''He saw her grow up. Our estates march together. It's just that he's been out of the country for the past eight years and

12

would expect to find her changed. And I suppose you two do look a bit alike." This notion did not seem to please him. "So, it was a perfectly normal mistake for the Honorable Fitzhugh Denholm to make. What was not normal was for you to allow him to continue under such a misapprehension. I call that low, miss."

"Oh, do you, sir?" They were at daggers drawn now and no mistake. Neither the avuncular tie nor the gray hairs that ringed his shiny pate could put a damper on her anger. "Well, I won't waste my breath any longer trying to convince you of my innocence. But if you insist on putting the worst possible interpretation on my encounter with the future baron, let me give you this to chew on, Uncle. Just what would you be saying to me if I had accepted his nibs's so-called proposal? There, I thought that might overset you. Well, now, sir, if you continue to treat me in this high-handed fashion, I might just send word to the Honorable Lunatic that I've changed my mind and will marry him after all."

"Oh, my God!" Sir Edwin, poleaxed, collapsed back down upon his chair, groping for a handkerchief to blot the heads of perspiration that had erupted on his forehead. And his niece, recognizing the perfect exit line once she'd uttered it, went sweeping from the room with her head held high.

This lofty attitude made vision difficult. Antonia collided with her cousin, who'd been kneeling by the keyhole. "Shhh!" Rosamond put a finger to her lips warningly, then grabbed Antonia's hand. She pulled her cousin upstairs and into her bedchamber, where she quickly locked the door and leaned against it. "We must talk," she whispered with a conspiratorial air.

"No, we mustn't." Antonia spoke at normal volume and ignored her cousin's "Shhh!" "At least, we aren't going to talk till you've ordered tea. And something to go with it, when it comes to that. I've already had two too many interviews this morning, and something tells me I'm not going to like this one above half either. Why didn't you go to the library as you were supposed to? No, don't answer yet. I certainly don't blame you for wishing to avoid that odious Mr. What's-his-name. But why did you allow me to walk straight into the lions' den, for heaven's sake? No, don't answer that question either. For heaven's sake, Rosamond, ring for tea!''

Antonia ignored her cousin's fidgeting and ate her way stolidly through a huge slice of nuns' cake and a ginger nut, washed down by two cups of China tea. Rosamond, jumping up every few seconds from the Grecian couch the cousins shared to listen at the door for footsteps or to cross the floor to peer out between damask curtains, refused all food and found little time for tea.

"For goodness sake, do sit down, Rosamond. You'll wear the carpet out. Try a ginger nut. They're quite delicious.''

"Oh, how can you eat at a time like this?'' Her cousin moaned reproachfully while plopping down again upon the couch.

"Easily. I need the fortification.'' Antonia touched her lips daintily with the linen napkin before replacing it upon the tray. "All right now. This should sustain me through your explanation. What sort of mare's nest have I stumbled into?''

Rosamond's story came tumbling out amid much handwringing and some few tears. Lord Worth, the county's most awesome aristocrat, she explained, had commanded his scapegrace son to return to England and reclaim his character by marrying his highly respectable young neighbor. "L-lord Worth thinks I'm the perfect choice for Denholm, don't you see, not only because our estates march together and Papa's rich, but also because no hint of scandal has ever been associated with the Thorpe name. And though the Denholm family is well above our touch in the normal way of things, Lord Worth says I more than make up for that by being so—so very—''

"Dull?" Her cousin hazarded a guess.

"Retiring. You see, no one would ever have heard of me, and we could marry and live quietly and raise a family." She paused to shudder. "And soon, so Lord Worth thinks, everyone would completely forget about Mr. Denholm's lurid past. But I don't believe that for a moment, Antonia. At least, I know I shall never be able to look at him without recalling it."

"My goodness." Antonia stared at her cousin with alarm. "What has he done?"

"What hasn't he done?" the other replied darkly.

"I've no notion. But I'd advise you to start naming the deeds, not the omissions, before I scream."

"Well, for the worst—at least, I hope it was the worst, for Papa wouldn't tell me very much and I had to pry the story out of one of the maids, who keeps company with a Denholm footman—he was caught, well, you know, in 'flagrante delicto' "—she was quite proud of the high-sounding phrase—"with this married woman. And then the husband called him out. And they fought a duel, and the husband almost died. And he and the woman had to run away to Venice." She paused for breath.

"And where's the woman now?"

"I'm not through." Rosamond gave her cousin an injured look. Antonia did not seem sufficiently impressed by this lurid history. But then, what could you expect from a soldier's daughter who had been reared abroad? "There's worse to come. This all happened years ago, you see, seven or eight anyhow, when the Honorable Fitzhugh was twenty. Anyway, the scandal had all but died down, and Lord Worth was thinking of fetching him home again. His lordship didn't wish to disinherit Mr. Denholm, who's an only child, you see. But then Lord Lytton—it was Lady Lytton Mr. Denholm had run away with—fell in love and wished to marry again. So he tried to get a parliamentary divorce, which fanned the whole scandal back to life again just when it was dying down. And then what do you suppose?"

"I haven't the faintest notion." Antonia's head was developing a tendency to spin.

"They found out that the Lytton marriage had never been valid in the first place. For Lady Lytton was already married to someone else. She'd been very young, and it was a secret marriage. He was a sailor and the thing didn't take right from the start, so they both just chose to forget all about it."

"How very convenient," Antonia murmured.

"Well, no, not really. For the bigamy came to light in the divorce proceedings."

"Well, at least it solved Lord—who did you say?—Lytton's? problem."

"Well, yes, in a way. But it rather made a laughing stock of both him and Mr. Denholm. All that fighting over a woman's honor who hadn't ever had any. And to make things even more complicated, the sailor suddenly inherited a title and a fortune that he had formerly been only third in line for. Or fourth, perhaps. I've forgotten which. But at any rate, he was definitely a long shot. Well, when this happened, Lady Lytton, as she'd been called, suddenly remembered he was the one she'd loved all along and went back to him."

"Poor Mr. Denholm," Antonia remarked with a total absence of sincerity. "Sounds as though he got his just deserts. But at least there's no light-o'-love now to prevent his picking up his old life again. The prodigal returns, and all of that. (She almost compared Rosamond to the fatted calf but fortunately thought better of it.) And his father's probably right. Folk will soon forget his history. So I expect," she opined shrewdly, "that there's more to your aversion, Rosamond, than just Mr. Denholm's past."

The other Miss Thorpe was deeply shocked. "More! My heavens, Antonia, isn't the fact that he's a rake, a libertine, a here-and-thereian enough?"

"Well, I suppose so," the other agreed doubtfully.

"Though, personally, I'd prefer his reputation above his odious arrogance. Still, they go together, I daresay."

"Well, I certainly could never marry a man like that," Rosamond said virtuously, then added with her chin quivering, "Oh, Antonia, do you think Papa will force me to?"

Privately Antonia believed her uncle capable of any sort of despicable behavior. But this was not time to be candid with her cousin, who was clearly terrified of the inevitable interview with her irate parent. Rosamond's fit of quakes might well prove terminal. "Well, at least Uncle Edwin's giving himself time to calm down," she remarked heartily, "and when he does, he'll doubtlessly think twice about forcing you into a marriage that you find so distasteful. You did acquaint him with your feelings, I collect."

"Well, I tried to. But you know Papa."

Again Antonia thought it kinder not to comment.

"I got no further than telling him of the attachment between Mr. Hollingsworth and myself when he went flying off into the boughs and there was no reasoning with him."

"Mr. Hollingsworth?" Antonia's eyebrows rose. "Ah-ha! I rather thought there might be more to this than the rakish Mr. Denholm's reputation."

Her cousin looked offended. "I can assure you, that is quite enough. Who would wish to marry such a man?"

"According to him, no end of females. And if he's as rich as you say and has a title in his future, I expect he was right in that much at least. Oh, by the by, is your Mr. Hollingsworth a curate?"

Her cousin looked astonished. "How ever did you know?"

"It stands to reason. No, no, I was only funning. As a matter of fact, Mr. Denholm mentioned that among his ravings."

"Oh, my heavens! Then, Mr. Denholm knows about Cecil. How awful!"

"Why awful? If you ask me, Mr. Denholm is your greatest ally in this matter. For he seems no more anxious for the match than you are. Less, if anything. Really I can't think what possessed the man to make his offer. He didn't strike me as the type to be forced into a marriage against his will. But it obviously was the case. For I tell you, Rosamond, he looked at me as if I were an insect. Anyhow, your troubles are over, for, believe me, Mr. Denholm has washed his hands of the whole affair.''

"But that's absurd. He hasn't even seen me. It's you he's washed his hands of.''

Antonia stared at her cousin, not believing at first that she was serious. "Oh, come now. He thought he *was* offering for you. And obviously he hated the necessity. Do you really think the sight of you would have changed all that?''

The question hung unanswered. Rosamond assumed a look of modesty while Antonia tried to assess her cousin from a male point of view.

It was easy enough to see how the case of mistaken identity could have happened. There was a strong family resemblance between the cousins. Both had fair hair, for instance. But Rosamond's was flaxen, Antonia's of a slightly darker hue. Rosamond's lovely blue eyes were ingenuous; her cousin's, as vivid in their color, had the disconcerting habit of seeing far too much. Rosamond's figure was smaller, softer; her mouth was "rosebud" as opposed to "generous." And if Antonia considered her cousin a trifle vapid, she was of the opinion that most gentlemen would find her otherwise. "Perhaps you're right,'' she conceded grudgingly. "Mr. Denholm probably would have reacted differently to you. But now tell me about your Mr. Hollingsworth.''

Mr. Hollingsworth and Rosamond, it seemed, had been meeting regularly in the lane, quite by accident, ever since he'd come to assist the local vicar six months before. The curate was handsome, sensitive, and very much in love. He was not, however, so Antonia gathered, of the required mettle to beard her ogre of an uncle in his den, let alone stand up against the power of Lord Worth. Mr. Hollingsworth was, in fact, prepared to play the martyr and lose his love.

Antonia fought hard to hide her contempt for such spineless resignation. It was easy to see from the love light in her eyes that Rosamond considered the Reverend Mr. Hollingsworth the perfect beau ideal.

"You could always elope," she offered; then seeing the shocked look on her cousin's face, "Well, perhaps not," she retracted.

"Mr. Hollingsworth is a *curate*." Surely Rosamond's tone implied, even a cousin reared in foreign parts should see the incompatibility of that particular vocation and an elopement. Her eyes brimmed with tears. "Oh, what shall I do, Antonia? Papa will get his way. I know it. He always does."

"Not if you stand up to him, he won't. He can hardly drag you to the altar, Rosamond. You simply must not allow him to rule your life to such a degree."

The only effect this stouthearted assertion had upon her cousin was to cause the tears to well over and cascade. Still, the exhortation to the troops was not entirely wasted. For Antonia recognized the promptings of her inner voice for what they really were. Let Rosamond quail and quake if that was her nature. But she for one, by Jupiter, was not going to remain in Kent much longer beneath her Uncle Edwin's autocratic thumb!

Chapter Three

When the London coach departed from the village inn the next morning, Antonia was on it. Leaving the Hall undetected had been no problem. Sir Edwin had been closeted in the library with his only child since breakfasttime, dictating her future. Antonia had simply put on her dove-colored lutestring pelisse with its matching bonnet, picked up her portmanteau, and trudged off down the avenue unobserved, her breath fogging in the crisp morning air. She'd left a note for her uncle with the inn landlord to be delivered after the coach's departure.

The Honorable Fitzhugh Denholm had not escaped his ancestral seat quite so smoothly. The interview after his return from Thorpe Hall had been stormy, with his incensed parent accusing him of deliberately antagonizing Miss Thorpe. "It was all arranged," Lord Worth, distinguished-looking and still handsome despite his years and habitual expression of discontent, paced up and down the library while his son watched stonily from a stance before the fireplace. "Sir Edwin and I had come to a perfect understanding."

"So you said. Unfortunately, no one seemed to have consulted Miss Thorpe's feelings. Believe me, sir, the young lady was adamant."

"You can't have behaved properly."

"If you're implying that I did not go down upon one

knee and declare my undying love, then you're right. Hypocrisy is not my style, sir."

"No, that's the one vice you seem to lack." The parent spoke bitterly while the son's jaw tightened.

"Even if I had played the part of the smitten suitor," Denholm replied, just managing to rein in his temper, "I don't think it would have made any difference. In spite of what Sir Edwin may have led you to believe, Miss Thorpe strikes me as a young lady who makes up her own mind. She does not wish to marry me."

"Well, sir"—Lord Worth stopped his pacing to face his son accusingly—"yours has been a spectacular achievement. You have brought the proud name of Denholm so low that even the daughter of a jumped-up squire—my God, the man's barely more than a cit—refuses to share it. And who can blame her? None of us will ever outlive the scandal you've brought down upon our heads."

"None of us? I can assure you, sir, that I for one do not intend to remain as encumbered by my history as you appear to be. I'm sorry that my indiscretions have caused you humiliation. Too sorry, in fact, since remorse made me override my better judgment and offer for a girl whose acceptance would have made us both miserable. Thank God, she, at least, seemed to have some common sense in operation. Be that as it may, when you're cataloging my list of sins, do acknowledge the fact that I tried to please you—and with my usual lack of success, I might add. Now I intend to follow my own inclinations and go to London."

"To London! You can't be serious! Your appearance can only serve to revive all the old scandal."

"Then, let it. I assure you, sir, I'll be no more than a nine-day wonder before the gossipmongers find other wares to sell. And even if I have a longer run"—he shrugged indifferently—"I certainly do not intend to rusticate for the rest of my life in order to avoid being the subject of their drawing-room tittle-tattle."

21

"It's too much, I suppose, to expect the sort of conduct due your name."

"Not at all, sir." The Honorable Fitzhugh Denholm smiled crookedly. "As you took pains to point out when you summoned me back home, my chief duty is to produce an heir—legitimate, of course—to carry on that name. And since I've exhausted the only matrimonial prospects the neighborhood has to offer, I'm forced to look elsewhere for a bride. What better place to search than the marriage marts of London?"

After this painful session, Denholm's intent had been to leave early the next morning and avoid a further confrontation with his father. In this he was successful. He was not quite early enough, though, to avoid his mother's tearful farewell. Lady Worth's unspoken reproaches were far harder to bear than his father's haranguing. Therefore Mr. Denholm was in the blackest of black moods when he tooled his curricle into the yard of the Cock and Magpie.

But even had his disposition been sunnier, he probably would have paid little heed to the public coach just pulling out upon the highway with an overload of passengers jammed inside and the leftovers perched precariously on the top. Nor did Miss Antonia Thorpe, squeezed between a farmer's wife and a drawing master suffering a bad cold, bother to glance out at the "bang-up-to-the-nines rig" the latter had mentioned with a touch of envy in his denasalized voice.

She was far too busy having second thoughts about the rashness of the decision she had come to. What Papa would say about her flight from the Hall didn't bear thinking on. Nor could she be totally sure that her grandmother would welcome with open arms a grandchild she'd never yet clapped eyes on.

The letters that arrived from Mrs. Blakeney once a year along with some handmade remembrance for her birthday had always been warm, affectionate. Of course, Grandmother would be glad to see her, Antonia stoutly assured herself. Whatever had caused the rift between her closest relatives, it certainly had had nothing to do with her.

Major Thorpe had always refused to discuss his deceased wife's mother. But somehow Antonia had formed the impression that it had been her grandmother who had severed the relationship. For it was apparent from those annual letters that Mrs. Blakeney was a nabob. Major Thorpe had evidently married well above his touch. And the scandal of her only child's elopement with the second son of an undistinguished family had obviously been too much for Mrs. Blakeney's pride to bear. *But she'll be happy to see me, I know she will.* Antonia squelched her nagging doubts. *Blood's thicker than water, they always say.*

And ale more satisfying. Mr. Denholm was reviving himself with a pewter tankard when a hand clapped convivially on his back splashed some of its contents upon the oaken bar. "My word, Fitz, it really is you! Thought for a minute there I was seeing ghosts."

Denholm turned to look into the round, beaming face of Lord Thayer Edgemon, a crony from his schooldays. "Thay—you old son of a—what the devil are you doing here?"

Lord Thayer, it seemed, was also on his way to London. And after a brief résumé of each other's activities during the past eight years, the old friends strolled out into the inn yard together, where they stood for a moment, each admiring the other's cattle.

"You *used* to be a famous whip, Fitz," Lord Thayer observed casually, smoothing the soft leather of his driving gloves. "I expect wallowing in the fleshpots of Italy changed all that, though."

"You think so? And I was wondering if the Whip Club hasn't lowered its standards disgracefully since I've been away." Denholm's eyes flashed wickedly as he drank in the ankle-length drab-colored coat with the enormous mother-of-pearl buttons and three tiers of pockets that

23

marked his friend's membership in the elite driving club. "Care to try me?"

"Thought you'd never ask." Lord Thayer grinned.

And so it followed that two sporty curricles went tooling down the King's Highway in the London direction at a fast and furious pace.

The coachman saw them coming, neck and neck, just before he reached a sharp bend in the road. Quite losing his head, he cracked his long whip out over the backs of his four horses and took the curve too fast. Lord Thayer gained the lead and swept on past him. Mr. Denholm, cursing, pulled up his pair as the stagecoach rocked precariously, then slowly tilted sideways into the ditch, coming to rest against a steep bank prickly with hoarfrost.

The coachman, knowing where his interests lay, looked to his horses. It was left to Mr. Denholm to disgorge the passengers from the angled coach. He had at last succeeded in heaving a shrieking, overweight matron into a sitting position and had then tugged her along the seat and up and out the door, when, panting from the exertion, he turned back to assist the others and met fully the enraged gaze of Miss Thorpe. "My God, it's you!" he ejaculated.

"I might have known" was the tight-lipped reply. "You seem to have become my personal nemesis."

"What the devil are you doing here?" He lifted her from the coach, even in his preoccupation thankful for her lightness.

"I *was* traveling to London," she began bitterly, "until two irresponsible ninnyhammers decided to turn the highway into a racecourse."

"Now, look here. If that cow-handed coachman—" he began until the driver in question, along with the irate passengers, closed in around him and made Miss Thorpe's comments the highlight of his day.

Some time had elapsed, and his purse was considerably lighter, the contents having greased palms all around, before the Honorable Fitzhugh Denholm climbed back into

24

his curricle, envying the callousness that had enabled his friend to go barreling along, oblivious of disaster. He was just about to crack his own whip when his eyes were pulled back, against his will, to the stranded group of passengers. Miss Thorpe, looking very young and quite forlorn, stood at its edge. A slimy-looking character, a thatch-gallows if he'd ever seen one, was edging toward her. Cursing once more underneath his breath, Denholm dismounted. As he approached, the slimy one slithered away.

"Surely you aren't traveling alone," he said abruptly.

"Surely I am. Being new to this country, I was unaware of its hazards. No one told me of the maniacs upon the road."

Denholm chose to rise above her conversational level. "Where are you going?" he asked with resignation.

Her opinion of his mental faculties had been poor from their earliest acquaintance. It had now reached bottom. "To London," she replied carefully, distinctly. "This is the *London* coach you've just overturned."

"*Where* in London?" His patience was on short leash.

"Oh. Grosvenor Square."

"Come on. I'll take you."

"But I can't go with you."

"Don't be tiresome. If you wish to stay in this company, it's all one with me." He nodded toward the probable cut-purse who averted his ferret eyes. "Just hang on to your reticule."

Denholm, in the act of climbing into his curricle, heard rapid footsteps. With a notable lack of enthusiasm he jumped down to help Miss Thorpe up onto the red-leather seat, then took his place and sprang the horses.

They rode in stony silence for a while, the curricle moving briskly. She stole covert glances at his face. He was frowning in concentration. Something she'd said kept niggling at his mind. "What did you mean back there about being new to this country?" he finally asked.

25

Antonia gave a scornful laugh. "You still haven't the slightest notion who I am, now, have you?"

"Of course, I know who you are." He looked her up and down as though in confirmation. She found it rankled that he seemed unimpressed by what he saw. "You're Miss Thorpe of Thorpe Hall."

"I—you dolt—am Miss Thorpe of Brussels. That's in Belgium, in case you'd care to know."

He gave her glare for glare. "What the devil are you raving on about, Miss Thorpe? I knew you in leading strings."

"It's news to me if you ever did. If you actually even bothered, which I seriously doubt, to look down your nose at a neighbor's child, well, then, you saw my Cousin Rosamond. So now you know, you loose screw. You proposed to the wrong woman!"

Chapter Four

"I did what?"

"You heard me right." Antonia was suddenly enjoying herself. Riding in this fine equipage, breathing deep of the crisp, country air, was certainly preferable to the crowded, stuffy coach. What's more, she'd finally managed to plant a leveler. The starchy Mr. Denholm was reeling from the shock. His eyes were glazing over. "That offer of marriage you flung in my teeth was evidently intended for my cousin Rosamond. I am *Antonia* Thorpe."

"Then, why the devil couldn't you have said so?"

"Why the dev—that is to say, why should I have introduced myself? Never in my wildest imagination did it occur to me that a man would offer for a lady's hand without even knowing who she was. I took you for a bedlamite. As a matter of fact, I'm still not convinced—"

"How the deuce was I supposed to guess you were a ringer? Old Thorpe has only one daughter—who, so he said, was waiting for me in the library. I had the vaguest recollection of a fair-haired little moppet with big blue eyes. You fit the description. The two of you must look a great deal alike."

"Not that much. Actually, my cousin is a nonpareil."

"Fishing?" He sneered.

"No." Her color heightened. "Trying to make you feel regretful, I suppose."

27

"Well, you'll not do that. Your cousin could be the reincarnation of Venus for all I care. I still wouldn't— Oh, my God!" The full implication of his position had just hit him. "Then, I haven't been rejected. Well, it seems I've left in the nick of time. When my father learns of my mistake, it will be bellows to mend with me." His jaw set grimly.

Miss Thorpe was scornful. "It is beyond me why a man of your age—not even to say of your reputation"—she quailed a bit under the look he shot her but stuck to her guns—"should allow himself to be pushed into a marriage that obviously disgusts him. But let me assure you that my cousin desires the match even less. Though I don't think for a minute," she confided in a rush of candor, "that Rosamond will have the backbone to stand up against my Uncle Edwin. But it does seem odd that you should be so spineless."

"It might be just as well, Miss Thorpe"—he slowed down his team to rest it—"if you refrained from speculating about matters that are none of your affair."

"None of my affair!" she blazed. "How dare you say so? You made it my affair when you offered for me. Now Uncle blames me for the whole ridiculous situation. Just how he thought I was supposed to know you were coming to offer marriage to my cousin when I'd only just arrived the evening before and had never even heard of you, let alone of your intentions, defies all reason. It was Rosamond he should have rung his peal over instead of me. She not only ran away like a scared rabbit, afraid to face you, but she saw me walk into the library and didn't lift a finger to warn me away. But did my uncle raise his voice to her? Oh, no! *I* was the one responsible for ruining my cousin's prospects." She glared at a weathercock atop a stone barn that they were passing.

The Honorable Fitzhugh Denholm studied her thoughtfully, a look of comprehension dawning in his eyes. "I'm not usually such a slow-top, Miss Thorpe. But I have had

28

a great deal to occupy me—a rejected proposal, a row with my father, a reunion with an old friend, the race, the wreck; is it any wonder that I've become dull-witted? But a young lady traveling alone, with no baggage to speak of—break it to me gently, Miss Thorpe, for my nerves aren't at their best. Are you or are you not running away?''

"I would not call it that," she answered stiffly.

"Then, let me phrase it differently. Does Sir Edwin know you've gone?''

"He will when the note I wrote at the Cock and Magpie is delivered.''

"I see. Well, well, well. It's true, then. Miss Thorpe of Brussels is running away. That note should send your uncle flying up into the boughs. But it won't be a circumstance compared to the news that you've run away with me.''

"Run away with you? Whatever are you raving on about? No one in his right mind would think a thing like that.''

"Your uncle's bound to. You've just said that he already suspects you of deliberately intercepting his daughter's proposal. Now here we are, tooling off to London together. My God, I can already feel the noose tightening.''

"Well, loosen it," she snapped. "I'm no jellyfish like Rosamond to be forced into a marriage. Nor is my own father the toadeater Uncle Edwin is. He would never be so blinded by a title that he'd not care who bore it.''

"I think I've just been insulted, but never mind. Your words still bring relief. Now tell me, who is it you plan to visit at Grosvenor Square? You do have someone waiting for you there with open arms?''

"Of course." There was more conviction in her voice than she was feeling. "I'm going to stay with my grandmother in her town house.''

"I can't tell you how gratified I am to hear it," he murmured as he looked with narrowed eyes at the road ahead. "Damn and blast!" They were coming to a posting house, and he'd spied a familiar vehicle in its yard. "Thayer's waiting for me," he said by way of explanation for his

29

outburst. "Wants me to pay up now, no doubt. Well, he'll have to whistle for his winnings. It took all my blunt to grease the coachman."

"You actually wagered on that race? That's disgusting. How could you?"

"Oh, easily enough. It was money in the bank till your coachman lost his head and landed in the ditch." He turned his team into the inn yard.

"Oh, indeed?" Her tone was scathing. "It did not escape my notice that you were behind."

"Only temporarily, m'dear." He grinned suddenly, an act that changed his whole countenance and caused her to look at him curiously.

Lord Thayer was emerging from the inn, wiping his lips fastidiously with a snowy handkerchief as Denholm reined in beside his curricle. His lordship's eyebrows threatened to unseat the jaunty beaver he was wearing as he strolled toward them. "Wondered what kept you, Fitz," he remarked affably. "Might've known. See you ain't lost any of your old touch. Who else could go to the rescue of a coachload of cits and come up with a gorgeous bit o' muslin. Oh, I say!" He was pulled up short by the warning look on his old friend's face.

"I can see, Thayer," Denholm groaned, "that you haven't lost the knack of putting your boots in your mouth. Miss Thorpe, allow me to present Lord Thayer Edgemon. Miss Thorpe, Thayer, is the niece of my neighbor, Sir Edwin Thorpe. She had the misfortune to be a passenger on the coach that you forced in the ditch with your cowhanded driving."

"Oh, I say, Fitz." His lordship was stung by the accusation. "Don't call me 'cow-handed.' That coachman had all the room in the world to let me pass." Suddenly recollecting his manners, he turned quite pink. "Honored to make your acquaintance, ma'am. Pay no attention to what I said. Should have thought. It's just that Fitz here is noted for . . . that is, he used to be—" He grew more flustered.

"Your apologies are about as graceful as your driving, Thayer. Which, by the by, hasn't improved at all during the time I've been away. I was right. They must let anything into the Whip Club nowadays." He chose to ignore Miss Thorpe's face and kept his attention upon Lord Thayer.

"You've got no cause to be insulting," the other blustered. "Beat you, didn't I?"

"Technically, yes. But actually, without leaving all that mayhem in your wake, which of course you knew I'd have to stop for, you couldn't have done it in a million years."

"Fustian!"

"Oh?" Mr. Denholm's eyebrows now outdid his friend's for altitude. "Are you just blow, Thayer? Or would you like to put the matter to the test? We're about—what—five miles from the next crossroads? Would you care to make it double or nothing for the one who reaches it first?"

"What about her?" His lordship nodded toward the passenger. "Miss Thorpe, that is to say."

"Oh, she don't weigh much. And I'm sure she's game. Aren't you, Miss Thorpe?"

She was opening her mouth to assert that indeed she was not about to be a party to another disgraceful race on a public highway when he quelled her with a look. "See, the lady doesn't object, Thayer. So how about it; are you game?"

"Don't see why I should have to beat you twice," the other grumbled. Then his sense of fair play, egged on by a conscience troubled over ignoring the plight of the passengers in the coach, came to the fore. "Still, if you ain't convinced. Double or nothing? Hmmm. Oh, but I say, I've had a chance to rest me cattle and you ain't. Don't want you coming up with any fresh excuse, Fitz, when I beat you a second time."

Denholm was about to waive this objection when prudence intervened. Though he was confident of beating his old friend, he was not nearly as unimpressed with the oth-

31

er's skill as he'd implied. He already had the handicap of a female passenger. No need in making matters any worse. "You've got a point there, Thayer, and it's damned sporting of you to bring it up. What do you say we engage a private parlor and build up our strength with a nuncheon while the horses rest? I've had no breakfast, and I'll bet a monkey Miss Thorpe left without hers as well. Am I right?" he inquired politely.

Antonia nodded, while wondering just how much further dining with these two pinks of the ton in a public inn unchaperoned would sink her reputation. Oh, well. One thing was certain: It was impossible that she could meet anyone she knew. "You goaded him into this race," she hissed as her traveling companion helped her down and they followed his lordship into the inn.

"Had to." He grinned, speaking low. "Pockets to let. Unless you've a hundred pounds stuffed in that reticule you'd care to lend me. No? I thought not. I've little other choice then but to win my money back. It's play and pay, you know."

"No, I don't know. But I'm convinced that Uncle Edwin owes me a debt of gratitude for saving his daughter from a gamester."

"Thorpe knows well enough what I am" was the cynical reply. "You'd be amazed at the number of shortcomings these encroaching types will tolerate."

Though she'd tried to convince herself that it didn't matter, Antonia felt considerable relief to find the public parlor empty as they passed through it to reach the smaller one Lord Thayer had bespoken. But when they emerged, almost an hour later, after a sumptuous repast of wine-roasted gammon and dressed lamb followed by orange cream, she was not so fortunate. A half-dozen travelers, in from the cold, were huddled near a parsimonious fire. And one tall, handsome fellow with a profusion of dark curly hair and side whiskers was wearing the uniform of the Third Dragoon Guards.

He was holding his hands near the feeble flames, too intent upon rubbing some circulation back into them to pay attention to the threesome crossing the room, though others in the group did look curiously at the two young swells and their pretty companion. Antonia felt her face grow hot as she met the bold stare of one male member of the party. She quickly averted her gaze, which then rested upon the guardsman. Mr. Denholm heard her gasp of dismay and quickly stepped up to shield her.

His action came too late. "Tonia!" the military man exclaimed in a carrying voice. "Tonia Thorpe! Is it really you?" He started toward them eagerly but was halted in his tracks by a haughty stare leveled through a quizzing glass. Mr. Denholm spoke with icy politeness. "I rather think, sir, there has been some mistake. Lord Thayer, will you escort my sister to our carriage? She is, I fear, unaccustomed to the overfamiliarity that one encounters in public travel."

The soldier's face turned red. "I beg pardon, sir." He bowed stiffly to Mr. Denholm, but his puzzled eyes continued to follow Miss Thorpe's retreating back. "It's just that your *sister*"—he emphasized the word—"bears an amazing resemblance to a young lady whom I knew in Belgium. I fear I momentarily forgot myself. You collect how it is in a strange place. One is always imagining he sees acquaintances. A natural reaction to loneliness, perhaps? I trust I did not embarrass your *sister*, sir. Pray convey my apologies. I meant no offense."

"I'm sure none was taken. This is not the first time my sister has been mistaken for someone else." With a curt bow, Mr. Denholm followed his companions out of the parlor. The soldier, frowning thoughtfully, strolled over to the window that faced the courtyard.

"Friend of yours?" Mr. Denholm inquired politely as he climbed into the driver's seat next to Miss Thorpe and picked up the reins.

"I know him. He's in Papa's regiment," she answered

miserably. "Do you suppose he believed that I'm your sister?"

"He did if he's a gentleman" was the brief reply.

Miss Thorpe gave Mr. Denholm a hostile look. It was quite obvious that the upcoming curricle race weighed more heavily on his mind than her reputation.

miserable. Do you suppose he believed that I'm your sister?

...

Chapter Five

"What happens now?"

"Why, we run the wheels off Thayer's rig." They were maneuvering their way through the crowded yard toward Lord Thayer, who was holding his team with some difficulty out on the highway. "Think you can hang on?"

"I'm the last thing you should concern yourself with. My own prayers are for all vehicles and pedestrians unlucky enough to be abroad today."

"Just the same, brace yourself," Mr. Denholm instructed as he pulled his team parallel with Edgemon's.

Antonia looked dubious. The lightweight, open, two-wheeled vehicle was built for speed, not passenger accommodation. "Brace myself how?"

"Plant your feet against the rest. And if necessary hang on to me. But for God's sake don't get in the way. Ready, Thayer?"

"Go!" the other yelled. His long whip snaked out over his horses' heads with a pistol-like explosion. His grays responded with a burst of speed that was quickly accelerated by an echoing whipcrack and the sound of the other high-strung pair being sprung behind them.

"Catch me if you can, Fitz!" Lord Thayer called over his shoulder.

"Intend to, old boy!" Mr. Denholm whooped as Miss Thorpe screeched "Oh, no!" beside him. "My bonnet!

My bonnet has blown off!'' She'd loosened the strings during their nuncheon and neglected to make them fast again. "Oh, stop, do!" She tugged at the driver's arm. "I must go get my bonnet."

"Are you daft?" He shook off her arm, which had caused him to jerk the reins. His whip cracked once more to urge his team on and shorten the distance between the two vehicles. This accomplished, Denholm steadied his cattle down, content to follow six yards or so behind Lord Thayer's rig. Only then did he give Miss Thorpe his full attention. "I told you not to interfere with my driving," he growled.

"But I've lost my hat, you wigeon!"

"The devil with your hat!"

"I can't go into London without my hat! Surely you must know that! It's the only one I have!"

"Then, here, take mine!" He removed the jaunty beaver from his own black locks and clapped it firmly on her head. It came to rest just above her eyebrows. "Now, then, you have a hat. May I return my attention to the race? Two hundred pounds will buy any number of dowdy bonnets."

"Oh, will it?" she sputtered, unjamming the beaver from her head and with a quick, deft wrist flick sending it sailing. Antonia watched with satisfaction as the breeze caught the curly-brimmed hat, lofted it like a kite, then left it to come to rest finally on the lower branches of a tree. Mr. Denholm, too, had watched the flight. He now turned a baleful eye back on his companion. "Feel better?"

"Some," she admitted.

"Then, can we get on with this race?"

"You can try. Though you obviously haven't a prayer." Lord Thayer was urging on his horses and the gap between the curricles was lengthening.

"No? Just watch me." The whip exploded in the air. Unleashed, the team put on an awesome burst of speed.

Mindful of the driving arm this time, Miss Thorpe clutched the third one down of Mr. Denholm's five-caped greatcoat and hung on for all that she was worth. Both curricles were flying now. Antonia had never known such speed. The wind tore through her hair and stung her eyes. It was fearsome—terrifying—exhilarating—glorious!

The driver spared a thought for his passenger as he rapidly closed the gap between his rig and his opponent's. "Are you all right?"

"Oh, yes."

The tone of voice surprised him, and he glanced down to see that her eyes were shining with excitement. "Oh, famous! We're catching him!" she crowed. "Can you go faster?"

"Hang on for the curve." He grinned and threw a protective arm around her as they increased their speed and took the bend of the road upon one wheel. "How are you doing?" he yelled in a manner almost comradelike as they straightened out on a long stretch of highway with nothing in sight but the other speeding vehicle.

"Don't worry about me!" she whooped back. "Just catch him!"

"All right, then. Here goes!" He gave a shout as the whip cracked once more. His cattle responded. Lord Thayer looked back over his shoulder to assess the threat and plied his own whip desperately. But it was soon obvious that his team was spent. They did spring forward for a moment but quickly flagged. Thayer was cursing and whipping for all he was worth when the other rig came tearing round him with Mr. Denholm, hatless, handling the ribbons with consummate skill while Miss Thorpe, in the same bareheaded state, shouted huzzahs of encouragement.

Lord Thayer, knowing he was well and truly beaten, slowed down his weary team to a humane walk while the rival curricle took another curve with only the slightest reduction of its speed and headed down the homestretch to the crossroads.

"Oh, we've won! We've won! We've won!" Antonia chortled, bouncing up and down on the red leather seat in her exuberance. "I never thought we stood a chance, and we've beaten him to a standstill. Oh, you really are a none-such! I'd no idea what a curricle race would be like. I tell you, it was famous!" She looked up at the grinning Mr. Denholm with glowing eyes. Finding her enthusiasm irresistible, he enfolded her into his arms before he realized what he was up to, crushed her against his greatcoat, and indulged in a victory kiss that began platonically enough but soon heated up into a great deal more than he'd bargained for.

"Oh, my goodness," Miss Thorpe gasped when he'd finally released her. Her cheeks were now flushed from more cause than just the cold. Completely flustered, she reached up to straighten the bonnet that wasn't there. "Oh, dear heavens!" The full realization of the depths to which she'd sunk now hit her.

Denholm, the thrill of victory now overridden by the strong desire to kick himself, watched her expressive face change from bewilderment to mortification. "I'm sorry," he said abruptly. "I should not have done that. Put it down to the exhilaration of the race. And, pray, do not refine upon it."

"Oh, I won't." Her voice was so earnest that he looked at her sharply as he picked up the reins and flicked them lightly. She caught the look and elaborated. "I have not forgotten, except there for just a bit perhaps, that you are a rake."

His smile was a bit grim. "You do believe in plain speaking, don't you, Miss Thorpe?"

"Oh, is it wrong for me to use the term? Then, I beg pardon. But I was led to believe that gentlemen were rather proud of that sort of reputation. Should I rather have said 'I know you are a devil with the ladies, sir'?"

"You rather should keep quiet," he growled, and gave his full attention to his driving.

Antonia had no trouble complying with that directive, for they were approaching the metropolis, and she was caught up in the sights and sounds and smells of London. Aware of her wide-eyed absorption and disdainful of the rude remarks of other drivers forced to maneuver around him, Denholm pulled his pair to a halt on Westminster Bridge.

"Oh, perhaps you shouldn't stop here." The driver of a heavily loaded cart had just cursed them roundly.

He shrugged and quoted: " 'Dull would he be of soul who could pass by a sight so touching in its majesty.' "

"Why, that's Wordsworth." Antonia looked up at him in astonishment. "I would not have thought—" She faltered suddenly.

"That a rake would read poetry? We can't be whoring all the time."

"Well . . ." She tried to pretend she hadn't heard him and rose precariously to her feet to drink in the view. "It's certainly all there, the things he spoke of: 'ships, towers, domes, theaters, and temples.' " She wished Denholm to know that he was not the only literate person in the curricle. "But I wouldn't call the prospect 'bright and glittering.' And"—she wrinkled up her nose—"it certainly isn't smokeless. Oh, my goodness!" she gasped, and sat down suddenly as a phaeton sped round them too close for comfort, and their team jerked nervously. "And it certainly is not 'calm.' "

"No. Of course, Wordsworth was here at sunrise. And since I've no desire to imitate his example, I'll take his word for the conditions." He clucked at his team and continued the trek across the bridge.

Antonia turned toward him impulsively. "Thank you for stopping, though. I'll always remember this when I read the poem."

The sweetness of her smile totally disarmed him.

"You're welcome," he murmured, feeling suddenly like a very callow youth.

Antonia's few moments of carefree tourism proved to be short-lived. As journey's end grew near, she gave no more than a passing glance to the sights her driver pointed out. Carlton House and St. James's Park might have been everyday occurrences in her life. The truth was, her apprehension was growing at an alarming rate. When her guide at last announced, "Here's Grosvenor Square," he noted that his passenger had turned quite pale.

"It's elegant, isn't it?" she offered a bit unsteadily.

"None more so." Denholm frowned as he pulled the horses to a standstill and stared at the imposing house just beyond the iron fencing. "Are you sure you have the direction right?"

"Of course."

"Then, we're here. But I could have sworn—well, never mind." He jumped lightly from the curricle, looped his reins around a hitching post, then came round and helped her down. Miss Thorpe was staring apprehensively at the magnificent facade and smoothing her hair nervously. "Oh, you're quite past praying for," some imp prompted him to say mischievously. "Your grandmother will just have to recall you from better days."

"But she's never seen me before," Miss Thorpe confided as they ascended the three marble steps together. "I do wish I were at least wearing my bonnet." Then it occurred to her that Mr. Denholm's presence could prove more awkward than her bonnet's absence. "You needn't wait," she said dismissively. "I do thank you for bringing me here, but it's not necessary for you to stay."

"If I were sure of that, I'd be off in a flash." His face was a study in martyrdom as he reached in front of her and gave the knocker four demanding whacks.

It was Miss Thorpe alone, however, who came into view when the door opened a grudging crack. A slightly stooped, august, though ancient, butler looked Antonia up and down. His disapproving gaze then came to rest, or so she fancied, upon her unclad head. "Yes?" he inquired frostily.

"Is this Mrs. Blakeney's residence?" she asked shakily, quite overset.

"This is Lady Thirkell's residence" was the frigid reply as the butler prepared to reclose the door. He was diverted from this intent not by the heart-wrenching groan from the young female but by a strong hand on the knob that pulled it from his grasp. He found himself craning his neck to look up sideways at a young gentleman who made his own efforts at imperiousness seem pitifully second-rate.

"Perhaps you may know whether a Mrs. Blakeney lives elsewhere in this neighborhood. The young lady here was given this address."

"Would it be Mrs. *Claire* Blakeney that the young lady wishes to see?" The butler appeared to have had a revelation. "Whereas this is by no means her residence, that particular Mrs. Blakeney does, in a manner of speaking, reside here. What I mean to say is, Mrs. Blakeney is her ladyship's companion."

If it had not been for Mr. Denholm's firm grip attaching itself at just that moment to her elbow, Miss Thorpe might have seated herself suddenly upon the marble stoop, which had developed a curious tendency to pitch and yaw. Mr. Denholm's in-charge voice was also proving to be an added stabilizer. "You do tend to make some odd distinctions," he said to the majordomo. "Suppose you move aside and let us in. Then go tell Mrs. Blakeney her granddaughter's here."

Though, as Morton afterward informed his underlings belowstairs, there was something decidedly havey-cavey about the girl; well, he hadn't been in service all these years without knowing a gentleman when he saw one, even if the aforesaid gentleman did have the effrontery to show up upon her ladyship's doorstep without a hat. Cloaking his curiosity in the habitual dignity requisite to his calling, Morton opened the door wide and ushered the peculiar pair inside.

Chapter Six

A wide expanse of hall was encircled by ascending branches of a marble staircase that ended in a gallery running across the entire back width of the room. An imposing figure in black bombazine stood squarely in the center of the gallery staring down at them. "This will not do. Stay where you are," she commanded in a deep, imperious voice that the visitors automatically obeyed.

The surveillance continued for several seconds. Then the elderly lady turned, crossed the gallery, and headed down the staircase.

"Oh, God, why me?" Mr. Denholm groaned underneath his breath and leaned weakly against the door. With mesmerized fascination he and Antonia watched the regal, slow descent. The white-haired, white-capped old lady used an ebony, silver-mounted cane to assist her progress. But in no way did she exude dependence. She held herself rigidly upright. Her height would have been impressive for a man. For a female octogenarian, the effect was intimidating. As were the hawklike nose and the sharp black eyes that did not appear to require the quizzing glass that she now untangled from the mass of jewelry on her bosom and employed as she stumped her way across the hallway toward them. Antonia felt a profound relief that her companion was the object of this stare. The old lady's progress came to a halt squarely in front of Mr. Denholm. She faced him, eye to eye.

"It is you. Thought so," she declared. "Well, this will not do, Fitzhugh. It will not do at all."

"What won't do, ma'am?" Mr. Denholm inquired with resigned politeness.

"You know what won't do, you scapegrace. I'll not allow you to bring your doxy here."

Miss Thorpe gasped. Mr. Denholm's expression hardly changed. "You much mistake the matter, Aunt Kate. May I present—"

"Indeed you may not!" She lifted her cane and struck the marble floor with resounding emphasis. Then she turned her glass for a head-to-toe inspection of Miss Thorpe. Antonia's cheeks burned under the deliberate scrutiny. Her relief was indescribable when the glass again was aimed at Mr. Denholm. "What is going on here, Fitzhugh? This chit ain't Eugenia Lytton. Too young by half."

"I've been trying to tell you, Aunt Kate," Mr. Denholm began patiently but was once again pulled up short.

"So, you've taken to running off with schoolroom misses, have you sir? Well, I'll tell you here and now you'll not run off with 'em to my house. Take your lightskirt and be off."

"How dare you!" Antonia ceased to be intimidated and glared at the old crone.

"Oh, for God's sake, Miss Thorpe, don't put yourself in a taking, too." Mr. Denholm's patience had worn thin. "And, Aunt Kate, do be quiet long enough for me to present Miss Antonia Thorpe, Mrs. Blakeney's granddaughter. This old harridan, Miss Thorpe, is my great-aunt, Lady Thirkell."

The imperious glare had turned to shock. "Claire's granddaughter? This is Claire's granddaughter? Little Tonia? Oh, you have really done it this time, Nephew." She glared at Mr. Denholm accusingly. "This won't do, you know. Can't begin to tell you what this will do to Claire.

Kill her, most likely. Nobody's such a stickler in these matters as she is. No, sir! It will not do!'' She shook her cane in Denholm's face. "I will not allow it! You can't play fast and loose with Claire Blakeney's granddaughter. There's no two ways about it. You will marry the chit. Immediately!''

"He will do no such thing!'' Miss Thorpe followed this passionate declaration with a sneeze.

"No one has asked your opinion, miss. You have no say in the matter. It's Claire I'm thinking of.''

"Aunt Kate!'' Mr. Denholm felt it more than high time to take charge. "Could we please move away from this doorway? And will you direct that ear-pricked butler of yours to provide me with a stiff brandy—and Miss Thorpe with tea and lemon? I'm sure she's famished—and exhausted—and unless I miss my guess, she's coming down with a case of the grippe.''

"Serves her right. Traipsing around without a bonnet like some Covent Garden jade. You heard the man, Morton. In the blue withdrawing room. And I'll need a brandy too.''

While Antonia gratefully imbibed her hot beverage she kept wrestling with the sensation that history was repeating, that she'd lived through all this before, which really was the outside of enough. Once was sufficient, thank you. But as the tea partially restored her equilibrium she recognized the source of the disturbing feeling. The room *was* familiar. Her grandmother had described it minutely, from the blue silk wall hangings, to the black marble chimney piece, decorated with night emblems in gilt bronze, to the mahogany armchairs with gilt enrichments in the style of Thomas Hope. And what's more, Grandmother had claimed it for her own, whereas in fact she was but a hired companion.

Antonia struggled to keep back the tears. Whatever was she going to do? She'd burned her bridges behind her with Uncle Edwin, expecting to find sanctuary with a grandmother whom she'd believed to be a nabob. Now she had discovered that same grandmother to be little more than a betweenstairs servant. It was all too lowering. She'd be out on the London·streets in a matter of minutes once that old dragon got it properly sorted out that she was not her nephew's light-o'-love.

What a coil! She swallowed convulsively and felt Mr. Denholm's eyes upon her. The usually cynical blue gaze now looked concerned. She must be a pathetic sight indeed to trouble that cold heart. Denholm's speech, however, revealed the true source of his concern.

"First, Aunt Kate, let's make one thing clear. There's no question of my marrying Miss Thorpe." He held up a hand to forestall the storm. "You gave me your word," he admonished sternly, "that you'd allow us to refresh ourselves and then you'd hear me out. You're laboring under a grave misapprehension. I am not running away with Miss Thorpe to set her up in a life of sin. In point of fact, our acquaintanceship is but slight. She was on the London coach, coming to visit her grandmother, when it overturned. I was traveling behind it, and having previously met Miss Thorpe—her uncle's estate marches with ours—I felt it incumbent upon me to bring her into London myself. So, instead of casting me in the role of seducer quite so fast, you would have done better to think of me as a modern-day knight-errant."

What had begun as a derisive sniff turned into a sneezing spasm. When Antonia recovered and wiped her streaming eyes, the aunt and nephew were gazing fixedly at her. There was a decided warning in the gentleman's eyes. "The drawing master next to me had a bad cold," she offered by way of explanation.

"Beg pardon?" Mr. Denholm looked bemused.

"The drawing master. One of the passengers. He sat right next to me and had a bad case of grippe. I'm afraid I've caught it."

"I suppose you lost your bonnet when the coach overturned, then." Lady Thirkell was thawing noticeably. "For surely you did not embark upon a journey without one."

"Oh, no, ma'am. It matched my pelisse."

"I am pleased to hear it. Quite relieved, in fact. As I know your grandmother will be. Although one must make some allowances, I suppose, for any unfortunate reared abroad, neither Claire nor I would ever countenance a young lady traveling without proper headgear. Not in England."

"Nor in Belgium either, I assure your ladyship." Miss Thorpe ignored Mr. Denholm's odious grin.

"So you can see, m'dear, that such a solecism—bad enough in itself, but definitely compounded by arriving on my doorstep not only unchaperoned but in the company of a notorious rake—would count against you." It was now Antonia's turn to grin. She quickly hid it with a handkerchief as Mr. Denholm shot her a quelling look. "Your abigail, I take it, was injured in the accident," her ladyship continued. "An awkward circumstance, but under those conditions you did right, my dear, by allowing my nephew to bring you here," she observed with judicial condescension. "It's too bad that someone more respectable did not come along. But providence does not always provide in the way we'd choose. I trust no one observed your arrival here, Fitzhugh?"

"Oh, no, ma'am," Mr. Denholm remarked meekly, while Miss Thorpe, striving to stave off a fit of hysterical giggles, asked shakily, "May I see my grandmother, ma'am?"

"Certainly, my dear. Fitzhugh, please ring for Morton." Her ladyship nodded at the bellpull hanging next to the mantel. The prompt appearance of the butler suggested he'd been lurking in the hall. He was quickly dispatched upon his errand.

"I deliberately postponed your meeting until I was able to sort things out to my satisfaction. If what I'd first feared were true, well, it was my intention to spare Claire's feel-

47

ings. Your grandmother, my dear, as you will discover, is a lady of delicate sensibilities. I am dedicated to protecting her from the harsher realities one is sometimes forced to deal with. But now I can see no impediment to a joyous meeting.''

If Antonia thought privately that her grandmother's ''delicate sensibilities,'' as well as her own nerves, might be best served by conducting their ''joyous meeting'' in private, she was too craven to say so. Mr. Denholm must have been thinking along those same lines, for he rose to his feet. ''Well, then, I shall bid you both good day.''

''Sit down, Fitzhugh,'' Lady Thirkell snapped. ''You will do nothing of the kind.'' And to his great chagrin, he found himself automatically obeying. ''Of course, Claire must meet you. She does, after all, stand *in loco parentis* for Antonia. Or, as grandmother, is she *parentis* literally? Well, never mind. She must meet you, of course.''

If neither of the young people quite saw the rationale behind the ''of course,'' it made no difference. The time to demur had passed. For the door opened and an elderly woman stepped inside, then hesitated on the threshold.

In everything but age she stood in sharp contrast to her ladyship, and even there, she could have been ten years younger. She was small and dainty. Her face, while showing the ravages of time, still held some vestiges of a former beauty. Nor did she reflect any of Lady Thirkell's self-assurance. Instead, she managed, even while standing still, to appear quite ill at ease and fluttery.

''Oh, there you are, Claire,'' Lady Thirkell observed heartily. ''Do come in, my dear. I think you must recall all the talk about me great-nephew, Fitzhugh. The one who disgraced us all by almost killing that sap-skull Lytton, then running off to the Continent with his wife. Well, guess who he's brought here to see you.'' Rather like a conjurer successfully pulling a rabbit from a hat, she swept her hand in a dramatic gesture. ''This, my dear, is your granddaughter—little Tonia. Come all the way from Belgium!''

Mrs. Blakeney's lips parted, but for a moment not a sound emerged. Then "Oh, no" escaped in a breathy little sigh.

Antonia's grandmother crumpled down upon the Aubusson carpet in a graceful swoon.

In the flurry that followed, while Mr. Denholm scooped up the prostrated Mrs. Blakeney and laid her on the couch-form sofa, while the granddaughter vigorously rubbed the grandmother's wrists (having heard somewhere that such action had a restorative power, though heaven alone knew why), while Lady Thirkell waved sal volatile underneath her companion's nose, Antonia had taken it for granted that her relative's collapse was the direct result of being caught out in her deception. How utterly shattering it must have been to realize that her granddaughter now knew that she was a mere hired companion and not the wealthy lady of the mansion in Grosvenor Square. Poor Mrs. Blakeney's sins had found her out. No wonder she had fainted.

Antonia was soon to discover, though, just how widely this assumption had missed the mark. Mrs. Blakeney's eyelids fluttered open and after a moment's bewilderment her baby-blue gaze came to rest upon her granddaughter. She moaned a piteous moan.

"Here, drink this, ma'am." Denholm pressed brandy to her lips.

"Oh, no. I couldn't." She shrank away.

"Don't be goosish, Claire." Her ladyship spoke firmly. "Think of it as medicine."

The dose Mrs. Blakeney obediently imbibed was liberal. She sat up coughing, then turned toward her employer. "Oh, Katie, I don't think I can bear it. Not to go through the whole thing again. I don't care if he is your great-nephew—and well-to-do—heir to a title—above her touch. I simply cannot bear it. Speak to him. Or, better still, speak to his father. Lord Worth could threaten to cut him off without a shilling unless he does the honorable thing and marries my little Tonia. She simply must not accept a carte blanche from him."

"Oh, for God's sake!" Mr. Denholm exploded. "Do we have to go through all this again? As for you"—he turned angrily toward Miss Thorpe, who was trying to bring a fit of near-hysterical laughter under control—"you're no help." But in spite of everything he found himself suddenly grinning, too.

"There, there, m'dear." Lady Thirkell sought to soothe her companion's agitation. "No need to put yourself into a taking. It's not what you think at all. Fitzhugh being here with your granddaughter is the merest coincidence. Antonia was on her way here, and the coach overturned. He happened along and drove her to London. That's all there is to that. At least that's what they say." She gave her great-nephew a flick of her shrewd dark eyes.

"And having discharged my duty, I must be going." Denholm rose from a kneeling position beside Mrs. Blakeney. Firmness, he had decided, was his only hope of extricating himself from Grosvenor Square. "Your servant, ma'am." He bowed to Mrs. Blakeney, whose color, he noted, was returning. "Aunt Kate." He bent for a moment over his great-aunt's gnarled, bediamonded hand, then turned to Antonia. "Good-bye, Miss Thorpe. Enjoy your stay in London."

"See him to the door, m'dear," Lady Thirkell commanded.

"I know the way better than she does, Aunt Kate."

"Run on with him, Antonia." Her ladyship's tone did not brook further discussion. Antonia dutifully preceded Mr. Denholm from the room.

"I expect she wishes privacy to decide what to do with me," she observed glumly once they were out of earshot down the hall.

"Don't worry. She'll not put you out into the street."

"You think not? It's hardly customary to receive a companion's relations into one's house."

50

"But then, Aunt Kate is hardly customary. Beneath that formidable bosom there beats a heart of gold. I think." He smiled to lift her spirits, but her eyes were fixed upon the row of Thirkell ancestors that lined the gallery.

"Well, perhaps her ladyship will allow me to be useful in some way for the next day or two," she said without much conviction, "or for however long it takes to secure my passage back to Belgium."

"To Belgium? You can't be serious."

"Entirely. I will not go back to Uncle Edwin. Indeed, I don't suppose I could even if I desired it. Which I don't."

"You don't read the papers, then?"

"How could I? I've not had a moment's leisure since I left home."

"Then, you don't know that Napoleon's escaped from Elba and is raising an army in France? English civilians are leaving Belgium, not going there."

Denholm could have bitten his tongue the minute he'd passed on this bulletin, for Antonia looked stricken. Still, it was none of his affair. He'd already been entangled with Miss Thorpe far longer than he cared to be. Even so, he found it awkward to extricate himself.

"Things are bound to look better tomorrow," he offered awkwardly, and got a pained look for the platitude. "Perhaps not, then. But your Uncle Edwin's bound to have regretted the tongue-lashing he gave you. He'll be begging you to return."

She chose not to comment. They walked side by side in silence down the staircase and neared the door where Morton stood impassively. "Well, good-bye, then, Mr. Denholm." It was on her lips to thank him for his assistance till it occurred to her once more that he'd been catalyst to all of her difficulties.

He read her mind. "I'm sorry for my part in your troubles, Miss Thorpe. I assure you, none of it was intended. "Except," he amended, "for the curricle race that cost you your bonnet. That was a financial necessity. Too bad I had to put you through it, though."

She sneezed again, as if in memory. "Oh, no," she demurred, as soon as she'd recovered. "No need to apologize for that. It was the only truly enjoyable experience I've had since I arrived in this country. I liked it above all things." Suddenly her face flamed. Ensuing events had completely wiped the race's shocking finale from her mind. She sneezed again. "I d-did not mean . . ." she stammered. "You must not think—"

"I don't," he replied, looking faintly embarrassed also as he shrugged into his greatcoat. "Again, the fault was entirely mine. Well, good luck, Miss Thorpe." He bowed, more anxious than ever to be on his way. "My hat, Morton." The imperiousness of his tone was meant to cover his unaccustomed lack of ease.

"You were not wearing a hat, sir." The butler's gaze was not entirely free of censure.

Miss Thorpe's gurgle of spontaneous laughter was followed by another sneezing spasm. Denholm could still hear it after the door had closed behind him. As he jumped the three steps and raced toward his curricle, it did not occur to him to wonder just what it was that he was running from.

Lady Thirkell had made good use of the interval of time she'd arranged for. "Well, what do you think of your granddaughter, Claire?" she inquired as soon as the young people had left the room. "I should imagine she exceeds your expectations, though I must admit to being shocked when she came calling without her bonnet and with my scapegrace of a nephew in tow. But she seems quite well-spoken, nonetheless. And pretty, too. Reminds me of you, Claire, when you were young. But why am I rattling on? She's your grandchild. What do you think of her?" She sat down beside her companion on the sofa and gave her hand an encouraging pat.

"What I think of Antonia is of no consequence. The

52

question is, what must she think of me?" Mrs. Blakeney's eyes filled up with tears.

"Now, now. No need to put yourself into another taking. Even if I did anticipate it. That's why I sent Antonia from the room. To get our stories straight. I do wish you hadn't spun that silly Banbury tale. It has made things awkward."

"Well, I never expected to see little Tonia." A lacy handkerchief dabbed pathetically at her eyes. "And a girl ought to think highly of her grandmother."

"And so she shall. If I had only known you were supposed to be mistress here, I would have pretended—still, with me nevvy showing up here as well, it would not have done."

"It wouldn't have done anyway. Imagine anyone believing for a moment that you were my companion."

"Humph. Yes, I suppose you do have a point. Anyway, what's done's done. We must now decide—quickly—how we'll go on from here. Antonia, I'm sure, will understand and forgive your foolish desire to impress her. So, please, Claire, let matters rest there. Don't go rattling any other skeletons."

"But I can't deceive the girl! Oh, you needn't look so Friday-faced, Kate. It's not the same thing at all. For it's one thing to pretend to be other than you are in a letter, written out of the kindest of motives, to someone you never expect to see. Telling a falsehood under these circumstances would be another matter entirely."

"No one's asking you to lie, Claire." Lady Thirkell sighed, knowing that her usually placid friend also possessed a high degree of stubbornness. "I'm simply saying that for Antonia's sake I see no need for you to go baring your soul to her right away. At least, let the child grow to know you first. But quickly now, before she returns, what do you think of my great-nephew?"

Mrs. Blakeney appeared bewildered by the rapid change of subject. "Well, actually, Kate, I've hardly thought of

53

him at all. How could you expect it, what with the shock of little Tonia's appearance—all grown up at that. Somehow I've continued to think of her as a child.''

"Well, think of Fitzhugh. It's important.''

"If you insist, then, I shall try.'' She closed her eyes and frowned in concentration. "He is quite good-looking.''

"Of course. That has been half his problem. Go on.''

"Well, he was most kind about the brandy.''

"Yes, he was, wasn't he?'' Mr. Denholm's relative nodded approvingly.

"Though a little impatient perhaps.''

"A little. But then I expect it had been a trying day for him. I have a feeling that there was more to his and Antonia's encounter than they were admitting. But what other impressions did you get of my great-nephew?''

Mrs. Blakeney pushed her power of recall to the limit but came up empty. "Oh, really, Kate. I do have a great deal on my mind at present,'' she protested. "Besides, what does my opinion of Mr. Denholm have to say to anything?''

"Why, everything. You see, m'dear, I've decided that Fitzhugh shall marry your Antonia.''

"Oh, but—''

"Shhh!'' Lady Thirkell shook her head warningly. "I believe I hear her coming. We shall discuss this thoroughly tomorrow, Claire. It may take a great deal of doing on our part to bring the matter off.''

When Miss Thorpe reentered the blue withdrawing room just seconds later, she found Lady Thirkell smiling complacently to herself and Mrs. Blakeney looking quite thunderstruck.

Chapter Seven

Lady Thirkell would allow no awkwardness concerning Antonia's position. Of course she must reside at Grosvenor Square for the remainder of her stay in England. Claire's granddaughter should have taken this for granted. As for Claire, who feared she might have inadvertently given the impression that she owned the house, well, what could be more natural, since this was, in every sense of the word, her home? The title "companion" was merely a sop for her absurd pride. What she was, in fact, was an old and valued friend. "I lean on Claire. Depend upon her absolutely," her ladyship declared. Antonia thought that as preposterous a statement as any she'd ever heard.

"We'll have a comfortable coze tomorrow, dear," her grandmother had said at bedtime when she'd lighted Antonia to her chamber. So far, there had been no opportunity for a private talk. Lady Thirkell had taken control of the conversation during their dinner and later in the drawing room before tea and early bed. She had used the time to quiz Antonia about life in Brussels but had tactfully avoided any references to her arrival in England and her brief stay in Kent. Antonia could only be thankful for the reprieve. Tomorrow would be soon enough to air that embarrassment.

But, as it developed, she never got the chance to explain just why she had arrived unheralded upon their doorstep.

The old ladies were not early risers. Then, when they had finally dressed and breakfasted, there was the matter of the second footman, who was far too attentive to an upstairs maid, to be dealt with. Consequently it was afternoon before the threesome found time for a conversation. They had settled once more in the blue room. The elderly ladies had their needlework and had supplied Antonia with a tambouring frame and colored silks. She was steeling herself to explain why she had left her uncle's house in such a shocking fashion when Morton materialized to announce, "Sir Edwin Thorpe to see Miss Thorpe, m'lady."

"Oh, heavens!" Antonia gasped. "Not Uncle Edwin, here!"

"You do not wish to see your uncle?"

"Oh, no, ma'am. Yes, I mean. That is to say, of course I must."

"Then, Morton, show the gentleman in."

If Antonia had hoped for some miracle that might have soothed her uncle's choleric temperament, the hope died at the sight of him. If anything, Sir Edwin appeared more agitated than in their past encounters. And to make matters worse, his resentment and anger were overlayed with a new emotion. For as he surveyed the threesome, meanwhile tugging at his cravat to its detriment, he appeared ready to sink from sheer embarrassment.

The probable cause was that Lady Thirkell had riveted him in the doorway with an assessing stare that seemed to weigh his bright blue coat and red striped waistcoat in the balance and find his provincial tailor sadly wanting. "Antonia, m'dear, you may present your uncle," she at last condescended to declare.

"Your ladyship, Grandmother, may I present Sir Edwin Thorpe? Uncle, Lady Thirkell and Mrs. Blakeney. Oh, but I expect that you and my grandmother have already met."

Sir Edwin, becoming more flustered by the moment, accorded her ladyship a deep, obsequious bow. Then with his eyes still fastened upon that august personage, he nodded in the general direction of Mrs. Blakeney. "May I please have a private word with my niece, your ladyship?" he asked.

"Anything you wish to say to Antonia can be said before her grandmother and myself. I shall go even further, sir. It *should* be said before her grandmother and myself. So, do sit down, pray." She indicated a caned-seat armchair, and Sir Edwin obediently perched himself upon its edge. "I have yet to ascertain," Lady Thirkell continued, "just how it happened that Miss Thorpe was traveling to London in a *public* coach." She paused to shudder at the term, then added as an afterthought, "Perhaps you do not keep a carriage?"

"Of course I keep a carriage." He was obviously affronted.

"Well, then, Sir Edwin, I can only say that I am shocked. For not only is a public coach a completely unsuitable mode of transportation for a young lady of Miss Thorpe's station, it also proved hazardous as well. Are you aware, sir, that the vehicle overturned?"

"I am" was the grim answer.

"Well, then, I rest my case."

"And are you aware, ma'am . . ."—being placed so unfairly in the wrong was causing Sir Edwin to lose some of his awe for the formidable Lady Thirkell—"that I had no say-so in my niece's choice of transportation or in her departure from my house? Are you aware, ma'am, that my niece stole from my house in the early morning hours without so much as a word to anyone? In short, ma'am, ran away?"

Antonia looked embarrassed and Mrs. Blakeney shocked. Lady Thirkell's black eyes snapped with interest. "No, I was not aware, sir, of the exact circumstances of Antonia's departure. But I will say that I suspected something of the sort. Now, then, what do you have to say for yourself?"

"What do I have to say for myself?" he sputtered. "What do *I* have to say?"

"Exactly. Antonia's father, your own brother, sir, an officer in His Majesty's service, who at this very moment may be locked in mortal combat with our country's enemies—"

"My brother is a doctor, your ladyship."

"The principle is still the same. Your brother placed his child in your protection. And you, sir, have failed that sacred trust."

"I have done no such thing! Why do you think I am here, ma'am, if not for my brother's sake? And for the sake of the honorable name of Thorpe."

A derisive sniff conveyed what Lady Thirkell thought of such pretensions. He paused long enough to look offended and then continued. "I am here to fetch Antonia back to Kent. As you can well appreciate, Lady Thirkell, a certain association will not do. For that reason I am prepared to forgive and forget her abuse of my hospitality and accept her once more into the bosom of my family." He avoided looking toward the sofa where Antonia and her grandmother sat side by side.

Lady Thirkell chose to misunderstand. "Are you implying, sir, that Miss Antonia Thorpe would be better served under your protection than under mine? What impudence! And how dare you speak to me of the 'honorable' name of Thorpe? I'll have you know that the late Lord Thirkell's family had long been noble when the Thorpes were still sniveling serfs. And you think to add to Miss Thorpe's consequence by taking her back with you? The notion is absurd."

"I think your ladyship is well aware," Sir Edwin observed stiffly, "that I cast no aspersions upon the name of Thirkell. I think you are also well aware, ma'am, that the association I refer to is the one between my niece and"—again the head jerked toward the sofa—"and—er, *Mrs.* Blakeney. My brother has never acknowledged any connection between them and has trusted me to concur with his wishes in that regard."

"Then, your brother is as big a fool as you are," Lady Thirkell snapped. Antonia longed to add a setdown of her own and to deny her uncle's right to speak for her absent father. The problem was, she hadn't the slightest notion of what he was talking about. She glanced uneasily at her grandmother, who sat still as death, her eyes fixed upon her folded hands. "Perhaps it will salve the plebeian sensibilities of both you and your brother," Lady Thirkell continued, "to learn that my dear friend Mrs. Blakeney and I have decided that Antonia shall remain with us as my relation and not hers. It is true, you know. We are connected. Antonia's grandfather and my husband were cousins."

"I am well aware of that relationship, m'lady, but under the circumstances, I should not think—"

"Oh, I doubt anyone will bother to work out the genealogy," her ladyship broke in impatiently. "And if they should, well, you may rest assured that my consequence is sufficient to overset any number of worn-out scandals. Antonia, sir, will remain with us."

While it was plain that Sir Edwin found a great deal to attract him in that arrangement, he was not a man who shirked his duty lightly. Therefore, even though he knew it was next to impossible to relegate Lady Thirkell to a secondary role, he nevertheless made another attempt to deal directly with his niece. "Your father placed you under my care, Antonia. He would be much distressed to learn of your defection. For his sake I am prepared to forgive and forget any former unpleasantness that passed between us. And"—he held up his hand to prevent interruption—"I am prepared now to admit that I was out of line with some of my accusations. Upon reflection I can see how you might have misled the Mr. Denholm quite unintentionally." He seemed unaware that Lady Thirkell's black bombazine rustled at that name and that Mrs. Blakeney raised her eyes to look directly at him. "Though, you must admit that to all outward appearances it did seem to be deliberate mis-

59

chief-making on your part. No, please. Wait until I have finished. I have had a long talk with Lord Worth and we have both agreed that in our eagerness to form this alliance between our houses we have, perhaps, been too precipitate. The Honorable Fitzhugh Denholm had only just arrived in this country after a long absence. And as for Rosamond"— he groped for the right words—"well, as his lordship pointed out, she is quite young and inexperienced and inclined to be, err, intimidated by Mr. Denholm's, err, worldliness. Lord Worth thinks, and I agree, that she would be better prepared for marriage after a London Season. His lordship feels that a bit of town bronze would make her a more compatible wife for Mr. Denholm."

"Just one minute, sir!" Lady Thirkell, who had perhaps achieved her own personal record for silence, could contain herself no longer. "Do I understand you to say, sir, that Fitzhugh Denholm is betrothed to *your* daughter?" Her voice rang with disbelief.

"Not to say *betrothed* exactly," he answered stiffly. "There is, however, this understanding."

"On whose part, I wonder? But never mind all that now. Just please explain, I pray you, how all this involved our Antonia."

Her ladyship and Mrs. Blakeney listened spellbound while Sir Edwin reluctantly explained about the mixup of identities. At the conclusion of his recital Lady Thirkell whooped with laughter. "Do you mean to tell me the young nincompoop offered for the wrong young lady? Lord, what a farce!" She wiped her streaming eyes. "And did you accept, Antonia?"

"Of course not!"

"A pity. But do go on, Sir Edwin. I'm all agog to hear what scheme you and that pompous Worth have hatched between you."

"We have hatched no scheme, ma'am." Sir Edwin bristled. "We have simply agreed to give our children time to become acquainted before formalizing their attachment."

" 'Attachment'!" Lady Thirkell chortled. "An odd term to use when me nevvy doesn't even know the gel by sight. But pray don't let me interrupt you."

"I shall try not to, your ladyship. The point is, Antonia, that I have brought Rosamond to London to stay with her maternal aunt."

"In hot pursuit of Fitzhugh, I daresay."

Sir Edwin kept his eyes fixed firmly upon his niece and pretended not to have heard his hostess's latest sally. "Rosamond is to stay with her Aunt Lydia on Wimpole Street. Lydia will sponsor her come-out and has graciously consented to introduce you to Society as well."

"And just who is this person?" her ladyship inquired.

"Mrs. Samuel Whitcomb, ma'am. My late wife's sister."

"Mrs. Samuel Whitcomb. Of Wimpole Street, you say? Well, she can't be of any consequence, for I've never heard of her."

"Mrs. Whitcomb is a close friend of Lady Hartswell," he was stung into saying.

"That tradesman's daughter?" Lady Thirkell sniffed. "But never mind all that. I do agree that Antonia should make her come-out. Don't you, dear Claire?"

"I-I suppose."

"And it really would place too much strain upon us at our ages to do the thing ourselves. Don't you agree, Claire?"

"Oh, yes," the other replied faintly.

"Well, then, it's settled. Antonia will continue to reside here in Grosvenor Square with us. But we will permit Mrs. Whitcomb to bring her out. Along with your daughter, Rosebud."

"*Rosamond*. But—"

"I, of course, will supply the guest list. Mrs. Whitcomb will be quite useless in providing the kind of company Antonia should meet."

"I'm sure my sister-in-law will have her own ideas on that subject, ma'am."

"Well, then, it's up to you, sir, to dispel them. For you and I, it appears, need each other. You wish your daughter to marry Lord Worth's son. I wish, for her grandmother's sake, to introduce Antonia into Society. So I shall see to it that both young cousins are provided with the very pink of the ton, including the Honorable Fitzhugh Denholm. And after that, it's up to Rosalea to get her clutches into him as best she can. Pity, though, about Wimpole Street. Not really up to snuff. But can't be helped. Your sister-in-law has a large ballroom, of course?"

Sir Edwin nodded dumbly.

"Well, then, we're agreed. Antonia and your flower shall make their come-out at Mrs. Whitcomb's residence under my sponsorship. I bid you good day, sir." Lady Thirkell rose dismissively to her feet.

Chapter Eight

"Go to bed, Antonia."

Miss Thorpe looked up in consternation from the sneezing fit she had had on the heels of her uncle's departure. Clearly Lady Thirkell and Papa were of one accord as to modes of punishment. But she was not still a child, however.

Lady Thirkell was looking at her kindly, though. "I should have insisted you not leave your room today. We cannot afford to have you ill. There is far too much to do. So go to bed, child. I'll send Maud in with Dr. Twiton's Receipt for colds."

"Oh, but it's only a slight one, m'lady. Papa says—"

"Nonsense. I will not have you ill. To bed, Antonia." The ebony cane pointed toward the bedchamber. Antonia sighed inwardly and gave in.

It was not the maid, however, who appeared a little later bearing the remedy. Mrs. Blakeney drew a chair up beside the four-poster and saw to it that Antonia licked every last drop of the disgusting brew from the spoon. "I know it's nasty, dear," she said sympathetically, "but quite efficacious. It was my own dear doctor's recipe. Lady Thirkell swears by it."

High praise, indeed! Antonia suppressed a smile. "Oh, do stay and talk to me," she pleaded as her grandmother rose to go. "Really, I don't know how I shall ever pass

63

the time. And we've had no chance at all to become acquainted.''

"Yes, I know," Mrs. Blakeney appeared troubled. "And, of course, after all your Uncle Edwin's hints, I do owe you an explanation. But perhaps that should wait until you're better.''

"But I feel perfectly well. Oh, dear, I did not mean that you should—You owe me nothing at all, Grandmother. Please stay. We shall not talk of anything you don't wish to.''

Mrs. Blakeney sighed. "No, it's much like Dr. Twiton's medicine. The longer you put it off, the worse things get. So, if you're sure you feel well enough. I must warn you, though: You may find what I have to say distressing. And dear Kate will be most displeased with me for confiding in you, for she feels it to be unnecessary. But though I do bow to her superior judgment in most matters"—she smiled faintly as Antonia murmured "Who doesn't?"—"I think she's wrong in her belief that scandals eventually blow over. She is so high-minded herself, you see, that she thinks others are fashioned the same way. But in this one respect I do know the world far better than dear Kate does. And there's no diversion, Antonia dear, that equals drinking scandal broth. And while the latest *on-dit* must have the greatest claim, of course, no scandal worthy of the name is ever really buried, but only laid aside to be picked up once more when the proper occasion arises. Your uncle certainly gave us proof of that today.''

"My Uncle Edwin is a prig. A very brief acquaintance has taught me that. Believe me, Grandmother, I wouldn't refine the slightest upon anything he says. So we'll speak no more of it. I cannot believe you capable of any kind of scandal.''

"That shows a proper granddaughterly feeling on your part, Tonia dear." Mrs. Blakeney's eyes grew misty. "But though it pains me to say so, I fear you much mistake the matter. The odd thing is, I never felt at all scandalous while your grandfather was alive. Not at any time. That was very wicked of me, I suppose, but there it was. Your grandfather was such a tender, loving man, you see. And so protective of us. I collect that's why I never felt at all like any of those terrible things women in my position are called. He was my true husband, you see, dear, in all save ceremony."

"You and Grandfather weren't married!" The shocked words popped out before Antonia could stop them. "I mean to say, how very interesting." She tried valiantly to erase the stricken look from her grandmother's face.

"No, Antonia, we never married. He already was, you see. And there was nothing to be done about that fact. It was a marriage of convenience, nothing more. His legal wife did not care for him. John and I had a house in Henrietta Street for twenty years and were completely happy. He was, as I said, the kindest, most considerate, of men. He died soon after your mother and father married. And "—she seemed in danger of breaking down completely—"though I know he'd intended to take care of me, it appeared no provision had been made. Kate, of course, is of the opinion that John's family simply ignored his wishes. She urged me to hire a lawyer. But I could not bear to drag John's name through the mud that way." She rose to pour a glass of water from the pitcher on the washstand and hand it to Antonia. "Your body needs fluids, dear." Realizing the real need was for Mrs. Blakeney to collect herself, Antonia obediently drained the glass. Her grandmother replaced it and continued her narrative.

"That was when her ladyship took me on as her companion. She was widowed, too, you see. Lord Thirkell and John were cousins and had been very close. Like brothers, actually. Anyhow, Kate insisted that I come stay with her. The way she put it was 'the thought of John turning in his grave over his family's treatment of you is making me positively giddy.' " She smiled wanly at the remembrance. "Of course, the Thirkell family was outraged. Dear Kate

65

considered that ample payment, she said, for her charity to me. For John had been the only member of her husband's family she could abide. Well, now, Antonia, the family skeleton that your father and uncle were at such pains to hide from you is out of the closet, I'm sorry to say. I hope you are not too shocked.''

"If you are the best the family can dish up in the way of skeletons, Grandmother, I shall consider myself fortunate indeed,'' Antonia said stoutly, hoping to hide the fact she was reeling from the blow. "Thank you for telling me. Now let's consider it forgotten.''

"No, no, dear,'' Mrs. Blakeney said sadly, "that is the point I've been trying to make. It will not be forgotten. Oh, Kate is right in one respect. Her consequence will override most social obstacles for you. She possesses one of the largest fortunes in London, you see. She was wealthy in her own right when Thirkell married her, and he was very plump in the pocket. And both their families are old besides. So, you may be sure that her cards of invitation will be coveted, even though she hasn't gone out in Society for years now. And the ton will accept you as her relation regardless of which side of the blanket you come from.'' Antonia flinched, and her grandmother looked stricken. "I know, my dear. That phrase is quite unkind. But I wish to prepare you for the sort of whispering you'll hear. For there will be talk. There's no getting away from that.''

"As if I'd care a fig.'' Antonia tossed her head, trying to make up for her initial reaction.

"Oh, one does care. One tries to tell oneself it does not matter. But it's galling to have one's character torn to shreds by people who haven't the slightest notion of your circumstances.''

"Oh, Grandmother. It must have been terrible for you.''

"No, no. As I said, your grandfather was the kindest— most protective . . . While he lived, my life was all I ever could have wished for. It was only afterward . . . Even so, I cannot regret anything for myself. I did grieve for your mother's position. For your father was never really comfortable with the situation. And now I am distressed that you should have to be made . . . uncomfortable.''

"I shan't be, I assure you.''

"It's quite all right for you to feel censorious, Tonia dear.'' Her voice was gentle. "For I wish to speak of something that will sound most odd, not even to say hypocritical, coming as it does from me. Whereas for myself I would not wish away the time I spent—under any circumstances—with John, it's impossible for me to lay too great a stress upon the importance of respectability. That is why I deceived you in my letters. I did not wish you to have any reason to feel embarrassed by your background. And I want respectability for you more than anything in the world. I want you to make a respectable marriage. Oh, I know you will enter the marriage mart lumbered by my character and your lack of fortune. But you have your uncle's respectability behind you. Sir Edwin may be a tiresome, pompous man, but, all the same, his character will help offset my notoriety. And you must not underestimate the value of Lady Thirkell's sponsorship. The combination of these two circumstances should, I believe, just about nullify the harm I've inadvertently done you.'' She paused to wipe her eyes.

"Oh, Grandmother!'' Antonia jumped out of bed and impulsively hugged her relative. "As if you could ever harm a fly. Don't ever say such a thing to me again.'' She, too, burst into tears. The two wept comfortably for quite a while in each other's arms.

During the next two days Antonia's case of the grippe flourished. Lady Thirkell insisted, over the invalid's protest, that she stay in bed. "It will pay in the long run. You'll see.'' Antonia was far too grateful to, not to say intimidated by, her ladyship to cross her. So she remained propped up in the huge four-poster listlessly turning through the copies of the *Ladies' Magazine* her hostess had supplied. "This should keep you occupied,'' her ladyship had said, "for you will need a new wardrobe suitable for the Season." Since the issues were hopelessly outdated, Antonia silently questioned their usefulness. But she turned their pages dutifully all the same. Would Lady Thirkell actually force her to make her bow in a gown that had been out of fashion for years? She shuddered at the thought but could not dismiss it.

When a maid popped her head in to announce a visitor, Antonia's surprise was overmatched by her relief from boredom. Who on earth? She'd barely had time to straighten her hair and fluff her pillows when her cousin eased into the room looking furtively around her. "Oh, thank goodness, Antonia, you're alone."

"Rosamond! What in heaven's name are you doing here?" The exclamation was hardly cordial. In the first place, Antonia was feeling little charity toward the cousin whose cravenness had landed her in such a coil. And in the second place, this was not the visitor she'd expected, even though the idea that her one London acquaintance might be concerned about her health was ridiculous in the extreme.

"I had to see you." Without removing the cherry *gros de Naples* pelisse she wore, Rosamond placed a cross-framed stool close enough to the bed for conversation, far enough away to avoid infection, and sat upon it. "Papa doesn't know of this visit. He has expressly forbidden me to come here."

"Oh? And why, may I ask is that?" In her short acquaintance with Lady Thirkell, Antonia had picked up pointers on toploftiness.

"Well, you must have noticed what a stickler for propriety Papa is. And he now says my character lacks stability. He greatly fears I'm easily swayed by undesirable influences."

"And just what particular 'undesirable influence' did he have in mind?" Antonia sounded dangerous.

"Why, your grandmother, of course. Which is absolutely absurd. As though I'd let her influence me in the slightest. I wish to marry Cecil, not to live in sin with him. Besides, I think it's beastly of Papa to preach propriety to me and at the same time plan to wed me to a depraved libertine.''

'' 'Depraved'?'' Antonia was diverted from her intention of removing her cousin bodily from the room. ''Surely that's coming it a bit too strong.''

''Not nearly strong enough. Cecil is convinced that Mr. Denholm is debauched.''

''Well, I must say I'm beginning to understand my uncle's strong objection to your Cecil. No one would care to hear his candidate for his daughter's hand termed 'debauched.' ''

''Oh, he never said so in Papa's hearing. Papa objects to Cecil because he's poor.''

''Yes, well, that would lose out to 'debauched' any day, I suppose. But before this conversation goes any further, Cousin, let's get one thing clear. You may tear Mr. Denholm's character to shreds as freely as you please. But if you say one more word that discredits my grandmother, or if you show her anything less than complete respect, I shall have nothing further to do with you.''

Miss Rosamond Thorpe's eyes widened with shock, then slowly filled with tears. ''Oh, Antonia, I never intended— I would never—while I cannot approve of—and c-certainly you could not expect Cecil to condone—a man in his position—a clergyman—but he'd never cast a stone—n-nor would I!''

''For heaven's sake, don't be so dramatic. I hardly thought you'd chuck rocks at her. I just want to make it clear that my grandmother is the dearest, kindest, sweetest person imaginable, and if you dare make her uncomfortable in any way, well, our come-out is canceled. My part of it, at any rate.''

''But that would mean that Lady Thirkell would withdraw her patronage.''

"Exactly."

The tears spilled over. "Really, Antonia, this is too unkind of you. I don't think I can bear any more. Papa is furious with me as it is. And now this will put Aunt Lydia in a taking. For she's been in perfect raptures over cohostessing with Lady Thirkell. She says that London's most tonish people will attend her party now. And that from then on her social position will be assured. And now you plan to ruin all that just because you think I shall be rude to your grandmother, which of course I should never dream of being. Really, Antonia, it is the outside of enough." She wiped her eyes with the fingers of her kid gloves and looked reproachfully at her cousin.

For some obscure reason Antonia felt guilty and, as a consequence, went on the defensive. "What actually was the 'outside of enough' was for your father to forbid you to come here. 'Undesirable influences,' indeed. If the whole thing were not so insulting, it would be ludicrous."

"That's what Aunt Lydia said. She said that in this case it was perfectly all right to disobey my father, for if he was too big a fool to know the advantages of being received by Lady Thirkell, she certainly was not. So, by all means, I was to come to see you. 'What your father don't know won't hurt him' is what she said. But I do hope he will not learn of it. Papa can be so difficult. Do take care not to mention to him that I've been here, Antonia."

"Since Uncle Edwin and I are hardly likely to be tête-à-tête, you worry yourself unduly. But was there any particular reason you wished to see me? In addition to calling in at Lady Thirkell's, I mean to say."

The sarcasm was wasted on her cousin. Rosamond merely looked grateful for the prompting. "Oh, yes, there is. I desperately need your advice, Antonia. What must I do about Mr. Denholm?"

"Do about Mr. Denholm? I'm afraid I don't understand."

70

"Why ever not? I explained it all before. I love Cecil. I cannot marry Mr. Denholm."

"And I explained that Mr. Denholm does not really wish to marry you."

"Oh, but he does. At least, it's what his father wishes. And Papa says Mr. Denholm's sure to wish for the match once he's seen me."

Antonia opened her mouth to argue that point, then closed it. She looked at her cousin's creamy complexion, glorious hair, limpid eyes. Perhaps her uncle was right. Gentlemen were not renowned for prizing intellect above beauty. Antonia found these reflections a bit dampening. "Well, you can always refuse him," she observed.

Such decisive action still had no appeal for Rosamond. But just as she was about to express her reservations, the cousins were interrupted by the reentrance of the maid, this time carrying a flowered hatbox. "This just came for you, Miss Thorpe." She placed the box beside Antonia upon the bed, then rather reluctantly withdrew.

"For me? But I did not—oh, Grandmother must have!" Antonia eagerly untied the string as Rosamond risked a case of grippe by daring to come stand beside the bed and see.

"Oooooh!" both young ladies gasped together as Antonia lifted the milliner's creation from its nest. The head-dress was fashioned in the style known as the "gypsy hat." It was made of British leghorn and ornamented with a full plume of ostrich feathers. Its saucy brim was turned up both in front and back. Its trim and ties were of deep blue satin ribbon.

"It's the most beautiful thing I've ever seen, not to mention owned." Antonia's eyes were shining.

Her cousin was too busy perusing the card that had fallen out upon the coverlet to comment. "Here's a replacement for your lost chapeau," she read aloud. "Consider it your part of the race winnings. Fitzhugh Denholm."

Rosamond stared at her cousin, openmouthed. "Antonia, the Honorable Fitzhugh Denholm has sent you a bonnet. Why on earth would he do a shocking thing like that? You must know—surely even in Belgium *anyone* would know—that it is most improper.''

"Oh, but you mistake the matter. I mean you mustn't think—Really, Rosamond, you are too absurd. It's not like that at all. Mr. Denholm is not *giving* me a bonnet. He is merely replacing the one he lost.''

As a rule, Rosamond Thorpe's mental processes were none too swift. Now she got to the heart of the matter with amazing speed. "You say that Mr. Denholm lost your bonnet? How on earth did he come by it in the first place?''

"Oh, dear." Antonia could see no help for it. She launched into a slightly expurgated version of the coach accident and the ensuing curricle race. The fluency of her recital was not aided by her cousin's increasingly scandalized expression.

When Antonia had finished her explanation there was a pregnant pause while Rosamond appeared to be thinking over what she had heard. "Papa will be quite displeased" was her considered judgment.

"Your papa will not hear of it unless you tell him," Antonia snapped.

"He will know when he sees the bonnet.''

"Oh, for heaven's sake, Rosamond, don't be absurd. How on earth would he know that Mr. Denholm bought this bonnet? But never mind trying to answer that, for the question's academic. I do not intend to wear it anyhow.''

Her cousin was still pursuing her own line of thought. "Papa was convinced that you were setting your cap for Mr. Denholm. I daresay he was right.''

"I daresay he was not!" Antonia replied with considerable heat. "I will not be held responsible for my coach capsizing. And how else, may I ask, was I supposed to get to London? Walk?''

"Really, Antonia, there's no need to scowl. I'm sure I don't mind if you have set your cap for Mr. Denholm.

Goodness, I've told you at least twice that *I* don't wish to marry him. But I really don't think you've much chance of fixing his interest. For I got the distinct impression that he didn't like you above half. Still''—she paused—''he did send you this lovely bonnet. Oh''—she frowned in concentration—''did I hear you say, Antonia dear, that you do not intend to wear it?''

''You heard me.''

''Oh, well then, may I?'' And before Antonia could do more than gasp, her cousin had whisked off her own black velvet headdress and had placed the gypsy bonnet atop her flaxen curls.

Rosamond turned her head this way and that as she preened before the cheval glass while her cousin seethed. ''You're quite right, Antonia. It is the prettiest bonnet ever. You're sure you don't mind if I wear it?''

''I most certainly do mind.''

''But if you're not going to—Really, Antonia, it does seem rather selfish.''

Antonia got a firm grip on herself. ''I am returning the bonnet to the milliner, Rosamond. Surely you must see that you cannot wear it any more than I can without explaining its origins.''

''But I can say I got it from you.''

''And do you think no one will wonder why I gave away such an obviously expensive hat? And what would Mr. Denholm think if he saw you wearing it?''

''That you were tired of it?''

''No! The thing is, Rosamond, as you yourself so effectively pointed out, I cannot be the recipient of such a gift.''

''I suppose you're right.'' Rosamond removed the bonnet with obvious regret. ''Propriety can be a nuisance, can it not?'' she observed as she carefully replaced the headgear in its flowered box. ''Oh, dear, the time!'' She counted along as the mantel clock struck three. ''Aunt Lydia is expecting callers and particularly wished me to meet her dear friend Lady Hartswell. I must rush or she'll be out of sorts. Oh, dear. We didn't get the chance to finish our discussion of Cecil and Mr. Denholm. I did so want you to advise me. I know we've barely met, Antonia, but I already feel fast friends, don't you?'' Rosamond was putting on her own discarded bonnet. "And you are much more worldly than I am. You do seem to have the most astonishing adventures. I expect it's in the blood. From your mother's side, of course. Anyhow, I'm confident you shall be able to advise me, the very next time we meet, on just exactly what I should do. Good-bye, Tonia dear.'' She hurried from the room.

Antonia sank back against the pillows and thought of several things she might tell Rosamond to do. Her gaze fastened on the hatbox. She took the gypsy bonnet from its container and stared at it lovingly a while. Then she slipped out of bed to go stand in front of the cheval glass and try it on. Perhaps the nightgown that she wore was to blame. Or the fact that her nose was still slightly red from her bad cold. Whatever the cause, the stark truth was, the bonnet had looked much, much better upon her cousin Rosamond.

Feeling far worse than she had at any time since her first sneeze, Antonia removed the hat, packed it carefully away, and crawled back into her bed.

Chapter Nine

Lady Worth's visit to her son's lodgings in St. James Street was ill-timed. The Honorable Fitzhugh Denholm had spent a late night at Watier's, followed by a visit to a barque of frailty and had been sleeping off the effects of both when his valet pulled the curtains to announce that his mother wished to see him.

He entered the withdrawing room some thirty minutes later, freshly shaved, wearing a deep gold dressing gown and a guarded expression.

"Fitzhugh, you do look dreadful!" his parent exclaimed, noting the bloodshot eyes, the pouches underneath them, and the way they squinted at the light streaming through the windows, evidence of a splitting headache.

"You don't appear top-of-the-trees yourself, ma'am." She was prostrated upon the sofa. A pretty woman, whose looks belied her years and gave no indication of the variety of ailments she was wont to suffer, Lady Worth had few interests beyond her imagined indispositions and keeping her irascible husband appeased. As her son suspected, it was the latter cause that had induced her to make the trip to London.

"Oh, I know I must appear a fright. The noise of Pulteney's Hotel was not to be endured. I did not close my eyes once for the entire night."

"You could have stayed here." A tea board lay un-

75

touched on the sofa table, the exertion of helping herself having proved too great for Lady Worth. Her son poured for them both and placed a Dresden cup in his parent's hand.

"Stay here? With you out carousing all night long? It is not to be thought of. And don't say I should have stayed with friends, for I am not up to doing the polite in my present state of health. I do not think you quite appreciate my delicacy, Fitzhugh. And while I do not like to reproach you, dear, the constant friction between you and your father is putting a dreadful strain upon my constitution. The doctor tells me that my heart—well, never mind that for the moment. The point is, only a matter of utmost urgency would have made me risk my health by traveling up to London. Fitzhugh, have you the slightest notion of what you've done?" The blue eyes, so like his own, looked at him accusingly.

"Lately?" he inquired, buttering a light wig.

"Please do not be flippant. Your father is quite beside himself. Fitzhugh, you have offered for the wrong girl entirely!"

While his mother proceeded to relate the matter of the mixed-up cousins, Denholm did his best to appear surprised by it. "How could you have made such a mistake, Fitzhugh? Your father is convinced that you deliberately set out to defy him."

"He mistakes the matter" was the icy reply.

"That is exactly what I told him. Oh, Fitzhugh!" Lady Worth pulled herself up to a sitting position and turned imploring eyes upon her son. "You cannot imagine how difficult living with Lord Worth has become. No one has more pride than he. You can never begin to know how dreadful all your earlier—escapades were for him. The notoriety!" She shuddered. "It was almost more than he could bear. Now all he wishes is for you to settle quietly in Kent. And Miss Thorpe—the *original* Miss Thorpe I mean, of course—seemed the perfect choice of a wife. Her estate borders on ours. Your holdings will be substantially increased. And while I'm the first to acknowledge that her background leaves a lot to be desired, well, as your father says, dear, you have placed yourself outside the social pale. No young lady of the first stare will have you."

"Oh, you think not?" her son asked dryly.

"I repeat your father's opinion." Her tone implied his words had been carved in stone. "But what I've traveled all this way to say, Fitzhugh, is that the matter can still be put to rights. Miss Thorpe has come to London. Miss *Rosamond* Thorpe, I mean. And please, please, Fitzhugh, do endeavor to keep the cousins straight from here on out.

"And while your father would have preferred for you to remain quietly in Kent, he concedes that perhaps this could prove advantageous in the long run. For when Miss Thorpe makes her come-out and the polite world gets the chance to see you form a respectable alliance—for no one is more respectable than Sir Edwin Thorpe, though I must own I find him a trifle too encroaching—well, you must see that it could do a great deal to restore your good name. And make your father comfortable once more. Then things could be back as they were before that—that—odious creature bewitched you into ruining all our lives. So, promise me, Fitzhugh, that you will do it."

"Do what, ma'am?" he inquired wearily.

"Dangle after Miss Thorpe, of course. Fix her interest. Offer for her again. Well, for the first time, actually. Oh, Fitzhugh," she implored, her eyes refilling with tears, "you owe it to your father. You can't know how his pride has suffered. As for me, well, I don't think I can bear his unhappiness any longer."

Denholm took a deep and steadying breath. While he had few illusions concerning his mother, he was fond of her. And though his father might not think it, he did have a strong sense of obligation to his name. "Very well, Mama. If you wish me to pursue Miss *Rosamond* Thorpe, I shall endeavor to do so."

"Oh, Fitzhugh, my boy!" Lady Worth, more animated than she had been for years, actually moved from the couch to throw her arms about her son. This tender scene was interrupted by the valet's entrance. "This just came for you, sir."

"Fitzhugh, that's a lady's hatbox!" her ladyship exclaimed after the valet had deposited the flowered container on a table and withdrawn.

"It's a hatbox all right, though as to its sex I could not say."

But his parent was already pulling the gypsy bonnet from its wrappings. "Oh, how lovely" was her involuntary reaction to it.

"Would you like it, ma'am," he said, and received an outraged look.

"Wear the headgear you've purchased for some lightskirt! Fitzhugh, how could you?" She tried it on almost absently before a convex mirror that hung between a pair of sconces on the wall. "Your taste is impeccable," she said, sighing, as she regretfully removed it, "which only proves the point I've tried to make."

"I'm afraid I don't quite follow."

"Well, you should. No *proper* gentleman, Fitzhugh, would have the slightest notion of how to select a bonnet that any female would die for. Your father could never do so, that is certain. It all just goes to show that it is more than time you turned respectable and settled down. And Miss Thorpe will make the perfect wife for you. Your father and I shall count upon your fixing her interest before the Season's done."

His mother's visit had made Denholm's headache decidedly worse. His blessed reprieve from an early betrothal had been short-lived. Well, he thought philosophically as he dressed to go in search of congenial company to divert the blue devils lurking to pounce upon him, if Miss Antonia Thorpe's judgment was to be credited, Miss Rosamond was a beauty at any rate. And then the memory of

Antonia's animated face as she urged him on to beat Lord Thayer and the feel of her lips upon his own rose unbidden to his mind. He wondered just what traits Rosamond might hold in common with her cousin.

"A gentleman to see you, sir." The valet cut short such unprofitable reverie. The unnecessary stress that Doggett the valet had placed upon the word "gentleman" somehow managed to imply that the matter was in doubt. Denholm finished his inspection of the *trône-d'amour* arrangement of his cravat and turned impatiently from the glass. "I don't wish to see anyone. Get rid of him."

But Mr. Burnside, who had anticipated just such a reaction on Mr. Denholm's part, was already in. He forestalled any impulse to throw him out by saying quickly—and unctuously, "I beg pardon, sir, for this intrusion. You must believe I would not impose myself upon you if I were not convinced that my business was of a nature that you'd be anxious to discuss. And, I might add, it should only take a moment of your time."

Mr. Denholm had been on the town too long not to know a sharper when he saw one. The tall, cadaverous-looking man seemed to be trying to ape the dandy set. His coat was tightly pinched in at the waist, its lapels enormous. But the inferior tailoring of this garment failed to conceal the layers of padding over narrow shoulders. His pantaloons also betrayed the artificial bulges over his skinny calves. Too fly by half and up to no good, Denholm mentally concluded.

"Have a seat, Mr. Burnside." He nodded curtly toward a chair and took another. "But pray state your business briefly. As you can see, I was just on my way out."

"Oh, I'll not detain you, sir. My business is the theater." He smiled ingratiatingly but, receiving a stony stare, continued. "I, sir, wear many hats in that noble cause: occasional actor, sometime writer, and now and then, producer. It is in these last two capacities I've come, sir."

"Look, Mr., err, Burnside," Denholm interrupted, "if

you wish me to put up the blunt for one of your projects, you're wasting our time."

"Oh, no, no, sir. Quite the contrary, in fact." His smirk was rather unpleasant. "Were you aware, sir, that Lady Hastings—Lady Lytton, as was—has authored a play?"

Denholm was too adept at cards to show his emotions now. The other looked a trifle disappointed when his expression did not change. "Eugenia? An author? You do surprise me. I had thought the lady could barely write her name. Or names."

"Well, in truth," the other acknowledged with proper modesty, "I did assist her ladyship with the actual composition. But it was she who"—he paused significantly—"furnished the plot."

"Well, that's all very interesting, I'm sure. But I'm due at my club." Denholm rose to his feet.

Mr. Burnside scrambled up also. "Pray hear me out, sir. It is to your advantage. As you may know, Lady Hastings has recently been widowed. And the late Lord Hastings's estate, while not impoverished exactly, is not adequate to support her in that style to which she has grown accustomed. And you, sir, would know more about that style than most." The silence that followed such observation caused him to speed up his narrative. "Her straitened circumstances have forced Lady Hastings to stop and consider all of her assets. It was then she came to realize the dramatic possibilities of her own history. As you know, few ladies of our era have had the fascinating love affairs that have enlivened Lady Hastings's brief career. And I can assure you that her adventures make good theater. Very good theater indeed. I'm confident the public will flock to see our production. By the by, we call it *All for Love*."

"Hardly original." Denholm sneered. "Now if you'll excuse me."

"But you see, sir, it did occur to her ladyship and to myself that what with the tremendous cost of theatrical production these days—hiring the theater, paying the actors, not even to think of the settings required and all the costumes—that it might be more financially rewarding *not* to produce our little piece, if you take my meaning."

"I think I do." Mr. Denholm was drawing on his gloves with the greatest of care, smoothing the soft leather over each finger.

"And Lord Lytton agrees, you'll be interested to hear. He has already become one of the play's backers, in a matter of speaking." Mr. Burnside sniggered. "Only he's backing it right out of Drury Lane. His lordship was especially concerned with suppressing the scene in which he catches you making love to his wife, as he then considered Lady Hastings to be. It's the highlight of the play, as you can well imagine." Again there was no comment. "But the more her ladyship thought about the matter, the more she regretted her decision to suppress a play that's bound to give so much pleasure to the London public. She's seriously considering returning Lord Lytton's money. You can appreciate, I'm sure, the artistic temperament. And the cost in pain of hiding a creative work under a bushel, so to speak. Why, it would be like smothering her own child."

"Now I can only hope," Mr. Denholm drawled, "that you are finally coming to the point."

"Oh, you're a canny man of business I can see, sir. The fact is, that even though Lord Lytton has contributed generously to the suppression of *All for Love*, Lady Hastings still would like to see her drama upon the boards. But if you, sir, who cannot be any more anxious than his lordship to find your most intimate history made public property, were to see yourself clear to matching Lord Lytton's contribution, I think then that the financial considerations would win out over the artistic ones. In fact, I will go so far as to say you can depend upon me, sir, to guarantee that Lady Hastings will have a change of heart."

"Does that conclude your business?" Mr. Denholm started toward the door.

"It only needs the mention of a sum. Five thousand

81

pounds is the going rate. Oh, naturally you needn't pay it all at once. We can work out terms to your satisfaction."

Mr. Denholm paused at his dressing room door and eyed Mr. Burnside with an expression usually reserved for the most repellent kind of crawly vermin. "Here, sir, are my terms. You can tell Eugenia to do her play and be damned."

Mr. Burnside, smarting from failure, left Mr. Denholm's lodgings upon that gentleman's heels and watched him drive away in his smart curricle. The entrepreneur could perhaps have profited by observing at that moment the technique of Captain Horatio Crosland of His Majesty's Third Dragoon Guards. The captain had just followed Miss Antonia Thorpe to Noble's Circulating Library wherein he behaved so charmingly, and referred to seeing her traveling alone with a certain notorious gentleman so obliquely, and assured her so quickly that her secret was safe as the Bank of England with him—her father in particular would never hear of it—that when Captain Crosland wrangled an invitation to the come-out ball, which was the talk of the town, he informed her, Antonia was scarcely aware she was being black-mailed at all.

Chapter Ten

As far as Antonia was concerned, the only circumstance to mar her come-out was the fact that her grandmother would not be present. When she had declared, "I will not go if you don't," Mrs. Blakeney, with uncharacteristic asperity had said, "Don't be absurd." And Lady Thirkell, when appealed to, had agreed. "Claire is right. It would not do. Your social assets are questionable enough without uncovering ancient scandals."

But it was Mrs. Blakeney who supervised Antonia's toilette and, as her ladyship's ancient dresser rebrushed one of the blond ringlets that dangled before the debutante's well-shaped ears, declared with misty eyes, "My dear, you are a vision. You will easily be the loveliest female there."

Though she smiled at the exaggeration, Antonia, too, was pleased with herself. Her fears that she would be presented in a gown that had been all the crack during the last century had been unfounded. Her ladyship had consulted London's most fashionable modiste and allowed the Frenchwoman to hold sway. "Simplicity!" had been the decree. "The young lady has youth, beauty. We shall not detract." The modiste had chosen spider gauze of a delicate blue, liberally tamboured with silver that sparkled by candlelight. Tiny white silk roses ornamented the shoulders over the small puffed sleeves. A wreath of the same flowers formed Antonia's headdress. White kid gloves and white corded silk shoes completed the ensemble.

There was a slight altercation over jewelry. Lady Thirkell's generous inclination was to adorn her protégée with one of her own diamond necklaces, a heavy ornate affair that Mrs. Blakeney and the dresser both insisted detracted from the ethereal effect that had been created. For once, Lady Thirkell allowed herself to be overruled. Antonia was delighted to wear a small string of pearls, a gift from her grandfather to her grandmother. She herself supplied the tiny pearl drops to dangle from her ears.

Lady Thirkell had taken unaccustomed pains with her own appearance. She had forgone her usual black and was resplendent in lavender satin worn over a gold slip. An opera comb branched out above an elaborate knot of her still-abundant hair. Now, to the profusion of other jewels that she wore, she added the diamond necklace. "We'd best leave," she said when she'd regally accepted Antonia's compliments on her appearance. "I wish to view the ballroom before the guests arrive. Heaven knows what that vulgar Mrs. Whitcomb may have done."

Her ladyship found very little to displease her, though, in the decor of the ballroom at Wimpole Street. She had already overridden Mrs. Whitcomb's desire to convert the room into a huge tent of purple silk, to suggest a sultan's harem. And though piqued by the disdainful sniff that had followed her suggestion, Mrs. Whitcomb had been too overawed by her ladyship's consequence to protest her scheme's dismissal. Now all Lady Thirkell felt compelled to do was to have the footman remove the masses of flowers from the side walls and rebank them with the groupings at both ends. "There is always a crush when I give a party," she informed the offended hostess as she stalked across the parquet floor with her cane, intent upon rearranging the orchestra, much to the conductor's consternation.

Antonia had parted company with Lady Thirkell and

gone upstairs. And when she first saw Rosamond in all her splendor, her instant reaction had been a prick of jealousy, squelched immediately, but wondered at. Since Antonia laid no claim to beauty, she rarely felt any rancor toward those who did. She was honest enough, however, to admit to herself that Rosamond's predictions as to Denholm's reaction when he saw the right Miss Thorpe could have had some bearing on the situation.

But if Antonia felt cast in the shade by the other's natural endowments, she took comfort in the fact that her own ballgown was at least as pretty as the dusky rose her cousin wore. And if Rosamond echoed Lady Thirkell's taste by wearing a fortune in diamonds on her generous bosom, what did that have to say to anything? "Oh, you look lovely, Rosamond," she said sincerely as her cousin rotated slowly to allow her dresser to make any final adjustments that might be necessary. "So do you," her cousin replied, adding ingenuously, "I had not realized you were so pretty."

At just that moment the clock struck ten. The cousins clasped hands for moral support and went to join their elders and greet their guests.

Lady Thirkell had not overestimated her importance. No one who had received a card of invitation, unless confined to a sickbed or experiencing a family death, stayed away. And if many of the guests were impelled by curiosity ("I thought the old dragon dead," more than one person was heard to say), it made no difference in the actual results. The requisite crush had been achieved. Mrs. Whitcomb, wearing purple crape and a tall headdress of ostrich plumes, was beside herself.

Antonia took due note of the Thirkell power as evidenced by the ball's attendance and kept waiting for her ladyship to fulfill her second promise to Sir Edwin and produce the Honorable Fitzhugh Denholm like a rabbit from a hat. So apparently did Sir Edwin, up from the country for the event, for he delayed as long as was considered proper before personally leading Rosamond upon the floor. Lady Thirkell had procured an ancient viscount to partner her protégée. The orchestra struck up an equally old-fashioned minuet. The ball was underway.

Captain Crosland, resplendent in his dress uniform, was quickest of the sizable number of young men who were waiting to claim Antonia's hand for the following set. The captain was so obviously enjoying himself and so very desirous of amusing her that Antonia quite forgot the somewhat dubious nature of his invitation. And when at the conclusion of their country dance he asked to be presented to Lady Thirkell, she was happy to comply. Nor did she try to correct the impression he gave her ladyship that he was a longtime family friend. When she was claimed by her next partner to join in a quadrille, she left him chuckling at her ladyship's wicked comments on the altered hair coloring of a certain guest.

Time passed quickly. Antonia never lacked for partners. Nor did her cousin, who, after her initial nervousness, appeared to be having a delightful time. It was nearly eleven-thirty when Antonia saw Rosamond standing up with a tall gentleman who seemed to have overawed and subdued her once again. And then when the movement of the dance caused the gentleman to turn her way, Antonia saw with a sinking heart that it was Mr. Denholm.

No one else in the room looked quite so distinguished as he did in the prescribed white satin knee smalls and dark long-tailed coat. It was easy to see, Antonia concluded, how any number of women might have run away with him. He lifted his eyes at just that moment as though he felt her stare. She quickly looked away. And later on in the evening she pretended not to notice when he stood up with her cousin a second time.

Certainly that fact had nothing to say to the matter when, a little later, Antonia felt an overwhelming desire to escape the crush. This need for a few minutes to herself was due, of course, to the buildup of excitement before the dance

86

and the rush of partners during it, both of which had left her exhausted. She eased out of the ballroom after a cotillion, dodged past the withdrawing room where her elders were playing cards, and found sanctuary in a small morning room, where she collapsed in a chair, nearly hidden by its enormous velvet wings. Antonia leaned back, closed her eyes, and for several minutes slowly plied her crape-and-ivory fan.

"Bored?" a languid voice inquired.

Her eyes jerked open to behold Mr. Denholm standing over her, two punch cups in his hands. "Here." He offered one. "I'm afraid most of it's sloshed out. Blame the pack of swains trying to follow you." He pulled up a chair, sank thankfully upon it, stretched out his long legs, and took a sip. "Aaugh!" He wrinkled his nose in distaste. "Lemonade! This is worse than Almack's."

She laughed. "What were you expecting at a come-out ball?"

"God knows. I haven't been to one of these affairs in years." The tone implied that it had been a deliverance. "But why the retreat, Miss Thorpe? You obviously are an unqualified success. And may I compliment you on your gown?"

"Thank you. And I'm not in retreat. Or bored. In fact, I'm having a most marvelous time. It's just that I felt the need to get away by myself a moment. Oh, dear. I did not mean—"

"Never mind." He smiled. "I'll not be so easily routed. I've done my duty manfully in there and am entitled to an intermission. And since Aunt Kate will skewer me if I try to escape before supper, you shall not monopolize the only empty space I've discovered. And speaking of suppers, may I take you in?"

She strangled on her lemonade. "Oh, no!"

"Is the thought that appalling?" he asked dryly. "I do occasionally forget my reputation."

"Don't be ridiculous. It isn't that. It's just that Uncle

87

Edwin would think the worst. And he's just coming round to halfway believing that I did not deliberately deceive you into thinking I was Rosamond when you came to make your offer.''

"Ah, yes, Rosamond." His face was enigmatic.

"She is quite lovely, isn't she?" Some self-destructive impulse caused Antonia to ask the question.

"Indeed. You did not exaggerate. She's everything you say. Tell me"—he abruptly switched the subject—"how does it happen that Captain Crosland is a guest? Aunt Kate tells me he's a close family friend. When he saw us at the inn, you gave me the impression you scarcely knew him."

"It's true. But he and Papa are in the same regiment, of course."

"But hardly intimate?"

"I couldn't really say." She looked uncomfortable. "I'm not acquainted with all of Papa's cronies."

"It just struck me odd to see him here. Tell me, was it his idea or yours?"

"Well—he did suggest it, I suppose. But it seemed the thing to do to ask him. Honor of the regiment and all."

"And the fact he saw you in my unsavory company had nothing to do with the invitation?"

"Oh, no," she said too quickly. "Of course not. That enounter, Captain Crosland assures me, is completely forgotten as far as he's concerned."

"Indeed?" His brows rose. "Well, Miss Thorpe, it hardly behooves me to tell you how to choose your friends. A case of the pot calling the kettle black you could say. But I'd be a bit wary of the ubiquitous captain if I were you. The fellow's a Jack Sharp or I miss my guess. Oh, by the by, what was wrong with the bonnet I sent you? Not polite to say so, but I thought it far superior to the one we lost."

"Oh, it was," she said earnestly. "And I do thank you for it. It was most kind of you. But of course I could not keep it."

"Why ever not? You're not making too much, I trust, of one impulsive kiss. I can assure you, the only strings attached to that headgear were its fasteners."

"I know that!" Her cheeks reddened. "I certainly did not think—"

"Didn't you? Then, I'm at a loss to see why you returned it—unless it did not suit your taste."

"Oh, but it did! In fact, it was quite the loveliest bonnet I've ever seen."

"So my mother said."

"Your mother? I don't understand."

"She happened to be in my lodgings when the footman returned it. And like you, she immediately thought the worst. Oh, don't look so alarmed. She didn't know I'd sent the hat to you. She assumed it was for some lightskirt."

"Oh, how awful for you." Her giggle robbed the words of sympathy. "I am sorry."

"You look it. I still don't see why you couldn't simply have kept the thing. After all, it didn't have a sign upon it, 'Purchased by the notorious Mr. Denholm.' "

"Oh, but it did. That is to say, it had a card, which my cousin Rosamond read. And she, too, thought the worst. So you can see that I had to send it back."

"Yes, I suppose so." He grimaced, then laughed rather wryly. "That's what comes of trying to make amends. It can't be done, as I should know by now. But I never expected such an innocent purchase to be so misunderstood. I'm slow to learn, it seems," he finished bitterly.

"Well, no one could have expected it to go quite so public." Her sigh was filled with regret for the ill-fated chapeau.

"Well, miss!" An imperious voice caused them both to jump. "I have been wondering where you were hiding." They had been unaware of Lady Thirkell's entrance. The dowager surveyed them, leaning heavily upon her stick. "This will not do, you know." But even as she scolded, she seemed slightly pleased. "Did you realize, sir, that you were expected to take Miss *Rosamond* Thorpe in to supper? Well, Captain Crosland has just done so, and Sir Edwin appears on the verge of apoplexy. At this very moment he's looking behind the palms and underneath the chairs for you."

"Oh, my goodness!" Antonia jumped to her feet. "Whatever will he think?"

"The worst, of course, if he finds you here," her ladyship cheerfully observed. "Oh, do hurry and claim Rosamond, Fitzhugh."

"Sounds a bit late for that. Allow me instead to escort you two ladies in."

"Not I, sir." Lady Thirkell smirked. "Lord Carstairs has that honor."

"In that case, Miss Thorpe, it appears you have no choice." Denholm offered his arm with mock gallantry and did not miss the reluctance with which she accepted it.

"Tell me, are we skulking?" he whispered a bit later as she tugged him into the midst of a large group of guests making their way toward the supper room.

"Yes," she hissed. "I'm trying to avoid my Uncle Edwin. I've already explained that he thought I'd set my cap for you. I certainly don't want to put him into that sort of taking once again."

"Don't worry. I intend to do my duty. Go join your cousin." He nodded toward a corner where Rosamond sat waiting for Captain Crosland to fill her plate.

It seemed that Antonia was barely seated, and her cousin had scarcely begun to exclaim over the great success of the ball, when Fitzhugh joined them bearing refreshments. And whether Rosamond's face fell because of the scant supply of food upon her plate or because of the plate's bearer, was anybody's guess. Then, when Captain Crosland materialized with overflowing bounty, he had no choice but to present one of the plates he carried to Antonia and sit down beside her.

The supper partners, thanks to the civilian outflanking

90

the army officer, had, at last, been properly sorted out. But the only person who seemed really pleased by the arrangement was Sir Edwin Thorpe, whom Antonia spotted beaming at them from across the room.

Chapter Eleven

The Honorable Fitzhugh Denholm had plunged into the life of the Bond Street beau, seemingly determined to take up where he'd left off eight years before when his celebrated affair with Lady Lytton had resulted in their hasty departure for the Continent. This social round included all-night macao sessions at Watier's, compensating workouts with the famous pugilist, "Gentleman" Jackson, trips to Newmarket to bet heavily on the races, and occasional appearances at the informal parties on York Street given by Amy Wilson, the stylish demirep. Interspersed with all these typical bachelor pursuits, he still managed a rather perfunctory courtship of Rosamond Thorpe.

It only took a morning call or two at Wimpole Street and a ride in the park during the fashionable hour, where they were observed by all and sundry, for the word to spread that the beautiful Miss Thorpe was as good as promised to her country neighbor, the notorious Fitzhugh Denholm. This made Miss Thorpe an object of wide interest. Each morning, cards of invitation piled up on the silver tray in the Whitcomb hallway. Nor did Rosamond lack for swains to fill the void when Mr. Denholm was otherwise engaged. The fact that the beauty was bespoken made her all the more attractive to the young men-about-town who might, had the situation been otherwise, have been afraid of becoming leg-shackled to her themselves.

Antonia did not fare nearly so well after their come-out. True, like her cousin, she was showered with invitations. Lady Thirkell's prestige assured her that. She was not, however, besieged by suitors. For the word soon spread that Miss Antonia Thorpe, while almost as pretty as her cousin, unlike her cousin, had no fortune. An early rumor that she was Lady Thirkell's heir died aborning when the social genealogists among the ton revealed that the relationship between her ladyship and Miss Thorpe was merely slight, if not actually nonexistent. "Fitzhugh Denholm," the gossipmongers whispered, "will likely be the Thirkell heir. Blood's thicker than water, after all, and Lady Thirkell has a *tendre* for rascals, besides."

Since Antonia had never rated her chances high on the marriage mart, she was not downcast by developments. Her London stay was merely an interlude, something to talk about when she returned to pick up her old life in Belgium. She was perfectly willing to spend most of her time in the company of her cousin, even when that company included Mr. Denholm. Though she thought it absurd that Rosamond still got the quakes in that gentleman's presence, she was glad enough to help her cousin over the rough spots. The addition of Captain Crosland to the group was also welcome. Antonia knew full well that the captain was too much an opportunist to be interested in her. But his easy charm of manner made him the perfect foil for Rosamond's shyness and Denholm's broodiness.

Therefore, when Mr. Denholm invited Rosamond and herself, chaperoned by Lady Thirkell, to join him for an evening at Drury Lane, the only surprise was that Captain Crosland, for whatever reason, was not included. And had she thought about it, Antonia would have attributed the silence that engulfed their box soon after their arrival at the theater to the ebullient soldier's absence. But she was too absorbed with looking around her to do more than note their party's heavy atmosphere.

The magnificence of the auditorium first claimed her attention—the elaborately carved half columns that flanked the stage, the gracefully curved four tiers of galleries, the crystal chandeliers that hung in such profusion. She was pleased that their box was situated on the side, so as not only to command an excellent view of the action on the stage, but to allow a full view of the auditorium as well. Her gaze swept from the orchestra, where the musicians were busily arranging their music sheets, on to the pit where the hoi polloi were perched on backless benches. She then shifted her attention to the balcony, where the pink of the ton were gathered, to see and to be seen.

Even Edmund Kean, the current rage of London, was going to have his problems competing with all this, Antonia decided as she ran her eyes around the boxes that sparkled with diamonds and quizzing glasses and glowed with the soft reflection of candlelight upon the variegated colors of satin and silk.

The audience was indeed resplendent. But Antonia found a silent satisfaction in the fact that their party had no reason to feel cast in the shade. Lady Thirkell's purple turban and the heavy emerald necklace she wore along with several ropes of perfectly matched pearls commanded instant attention. Rosamond looked unusually lovely in a white crape dress spotted with white satin and trimmed with bands of flowers and leaves of deep blue silk. She herself wore a gown of Urling's net over a pale pink satin slip. But, as always, she concluded, it was Mr. Denholm who distinguished their little group. The severity of his black and white evening clothes was perfectly suited to his inky hair, Antonia decided with something less than complete objectivity.

She was not as approving of his habitual hauteur, though, especially now that she had seen him abandon it upon occasion to become quite personable and human. But for some reason he seemed more toplofty than usual this evening, sitting in tight-lipped silence, seemingly unconcerned by any hostly obligation to his guests, his eyes focused on the closed stage curtain. Well, he was Rosamond's problem, thank goodness, and not hers. His moodiness was not going to interfere with her first taste of London theater.

Just as Antonia resolved this, she heard some timid remark of her cousin's remain unanswered. Even the ever-garrulous Lady Thirkell seemed to have lost her tongue.

Botheration! Rosamond's discomfort overrode Antonia's desire to be as boorish as their host. "Oh, who is that lovely lady everybody's looking at?" Antonia asked. To this conversational gambit she quickly added, "Oh, don't all turn your heads at once, for while everyone else is gaping at her, she is looking directly our way."

There was no need for this admonition. Denholm did not waver from his contemplation of the stage. Lady Thirkell had developed a sudden need to rearrange the numerous rings she wore. Only Rosamond appeared appreciative of Antonia's efforts to enliven their theater party. "What lady, where?" she asked.

"In the fourth box from the end, directly across. She must be someone quite famous, the way everyone stares. Royalty, do you suppose?"

The cousins gazed admiringly at the striking black-haired beauty, whose black evening gown was cut daringly low to expose a rather shocking amount of alabaster shoulders and seductive bosom. Small jet beads were her only ornament. Her hair was braided high in a coronet, topped with a green-jade ornament. Both Misses Thorpe felt suddenly quite young and gauche as they gazed at the sophisticate.

"Do you perhaps know who she is, sir?" Antonia was beginning to grow exasperated at the Denholm silence.

"Why ask him?" Lady Thirkell sounded waspish. "He's been out of London for years now."

"I was not so much seeking enlightenment as giving our host an opportunity to enter the conversation." Antonia immediately regretted the rash remark. It was just as well that at that very moment the curtain rose.

Edmund Kean's *Richard III* had dazzled the critics. He

did not have the same effect upon Lady Thirkell. Her piercing black eyes followed his hunchbacked progress for several seconds, then she was heard to sniff, "Looks like a monkey," and after an even shorter interval, "Sounds like one, too." Someone in the adjoining box was heard to titter. When Antonia next glanced at Lady Thirkell, the dowager was sound asleep.

Rosamond soon lost the plot thread, wriggled in her chair, and mainly watched the audience. Denholm might have been carved from the same stone as the Grecian columns from the amount of animation he conveyed. Only Antonia seemed caught up in the villain's powerful emotion, as she leaned out over the railing of their box to watch with parted lips and widened eyes. When the curtain was lowered at intermission, it took several seconds for her to return to reality.

Lady Thirkell shook off the spell of Morpheus far quicker than Antonia escaped the spell of Kean. When the curtain dropped, her head snapped up, and with the help of the ebony stick she carried she rose quickly to her feet. "Lady Mary Harlowe's here. Better go speak to her. That way I can leave when I want to. If she comes to our box, she'll prose on and on and never go away." The black eyes fastened on Rosamond. "Miss Thorpe, you can take me."

Rosamond rose thankfully to her feet. Intimidating as Lady Thirkell was, she dreaded trying to make conversation with Mr. Denholm even more. "Oh, not you, Antonia." Her ladyship dismissed the other Miss Thorpe, who seemed bent on accompanying them. "You stay here and guard Fitzhugh."

"What on earth did she mean by that?" Antonia blurted out as soon as the velvet box curtains had closed behind the two. She and Denholm were on their feet. They moved together toward the back of the box, where they'd be less conspicuous.

"Do you mind if I blow a cloud?" he asked abruptly.

She did but decided it was politic not to say so since he

might soon find her conduct equally distasteful. Still, she watched with undisguised disapproval while he pulled a cigar from the recesses of his coat and began puffing to ignite it. She placed a kid glove delicately over her mouth and coughed pointedly. The only result was that the blue eyes fastened unswervingly upon her face till the smoke he blew obscured them.

"It's just as well we're alone," Antonia said abruptly, "for I did wish to speak to you."

"What makes me suppose you're about to ring a peal over me? Your pointed remark about my lack of civility perhaps? I'm sorry if you feel I've neglected you, Miss Thorpe."

"Don't be ridiculous," Antonia snapped. "As if I care a fig about your behavior. It's Rosamond I'm concerned with. You've put the poor girl into a proper quake with your distemper. And just when she was beginning to feel more comfortable around you."

"I'm sorry if your cousin thinks me an ogre. But it was an opinion already formed before I'd met her, you may recall."

"Well, all the more reason you should be at pains to dispel it. You do intend to offer for her, do you not?"

"I think that question would be a bit more appropriate from Sir Edwin than from you, Miss Thorpe." Her face flamed red. "But since you ask, yes, I do."

"I beg your pardon." She managed to keep both her temper and her voice level. "I deserved the setdown. But since I've already sunk myself below reproach, let me go on and say that unless you are deliberately trying to goad her into refusing you—as you did when you believed that I was she—then I think you should treat her with more kindness. Rosamond, as you yourself have noted, is rather inclined to be overset by your, err, worldliness. You might try and be more considerate of that fact."

"And just what, may I ask, is your particular interest in the matter? Are you afraid—or hoping—that if your cousin turns me down, offering for you will have become habit-forming?''

"I realize, Mr. Denholm, that you are trying to be deliberately insulting and shall therefore overlook it. What I do not understand, though, is just what has put you in such a temper.''

Since he had no intention of enlightening her, it was just as well that they were rejoined by Lady Thirkell and Rosamond. Antonia's own temper began to cool when she noted that her rag-mannered lecture had not been wasted. Denholm was at some pains to seat both ladies courteously. He then proceeded to engage in small talk with her cousin. Rosamond was relaxed and smiling when the play resumed.

Lady Thirkell went immediately back to sleep. The Shakespearean drama had lost some of its power to enthrall Antonia as well, due entirely to her altercation with Mr. Denholm, she thought resentfully. So, when the play reached its tragic culmination and Lady Thirkell revived just as Richard the Third expired, she thought it considerate to suggest they leave. "Leave!" her ladyship exploded. "After suffering through all of this? Don't be sap-skulled. Only came to see the farce!''

Rosamond, too, was all eagerness. There was no doubt that for her as well the more frivolous portion of the evening's theatrical fare held far greater appeal than Shakespeare. Mr. Denholm, who had seemed more than willing to depart, settled back down once more with a contrived smile that signaled to Antonia: "See how gracious I am being.''

The farce lovers were doomed to disappointment, though, for the theater manager appeared upon the stage to announce a change in the evening's fare. Instead of *Devil to Pay*, as indicated upon the playbill, they were to be treated to a brand-new afterpiece, "never yet performed on this or any other stage,'' written by a brilliant new lady author, who wished to keep her identity a secret, and entitled *All for Love*.

Antonia, who had been covertly observing Mr. Denholm, seemed to imagine rather than see a look of consternation appear upon his face before it was wiped clean once more of all expression.

"Why ain't they going to do the farce?" Lady Thirkell complained to the world at large.

Antonia found the piece to be boring, too cloying for words. But when she looked around and saw the other patrons leaning forward, literally on the edges of their seats, giving this play a far more rapt attention than that accorded the brilliant Kean, she began to wonder if she had not allowed the accumulated fatigue from five acts of Shakespearean tragedy to cloud her perceptions. She returned her attention to the stage.

She remained mystified, however, by the general reaction, which was shared, she noted, by the other occupants of her box. True, the actor and actress upon the stage were personable. But the dialogue with which they declared their undying love and tragic circumstances seemed hopelessly stilted, if not plain silly.

Antonia squirmed a little in her seat and wished once more that they could leave. Small chance of that. Lady Thirkell, refreshed no doubt by napping during *Richard III*, was drinking in every word of the cloying dialogue, her hands clinched tightly upon her stick, her face suffering along with the pair on stage.

Antonia was less surprised that Rosamond looked stricken by the star-crossed lovers' plight. She was no doubt thinking of her curate. Antonia glanced past her cousin, expecting to find a fellow critic in Mr. Denholm. For, no matter what opinion she might have formed about some other aspects of his personality, she did hold his intelligence in high regard. Until this moment. For he seemed to have come under the spell of the maudlin drama as much as anyone. More perhaps. He was so intent and still as to appear mesmerized.

Completely mystified now, Antonia returned her attention to the stage, where the trysting lovers, locked in a passionate embrace, were interrupted by the entrance of the lady's husband with a pistol in his hand. How melodramatic. How predictable. How boring. Her eyes traveled aimlessly along the horseshoe of boxes as if seeking further confirmation of her judgment. Sure enough, she was not the only person in the theater whose attention now wandered from the play. In fact, more of the tonish occupants of the boxes seemed staring her way than were looking toward the stage. When the light then finally dawned, it was all Antonia could do to keep from gasping.

How could she have been so stupid! How could she have not realized! Why, even Rosamond was aware of what was happening. And she'd thought her cousin none too bright. She sank back into her chair, willing herself to become invisible.

The afterpiece seemed to go on and on forever, through duel, flight, and romantic exile. Antonia divided her time between wishing the balcony would collapse and end their misery and concentrating upon not looking Denholm's way again. One glance at his masklike face would most likely turn her into stone.

When the lovers on stage were finally wrenched apart by the heroine's sad recall to a higher duty, Antonia breathed a long, if silent, sigh of relief. They could soon leave this public box where they were pilloried. Rosamond was crying softly. From mortification, Antonia felt sure. And while she could certainly sympathize with that reaction, she did wish, for Denholm's sake, that her cousin could be more stoic. Oh, thank heavens it was finally over. The curtain closed to thunderous applause.

"Well, shall we go?" she asked, too brightly. "My bottom is quite numb. Oh, dear. I mean to say—" Her cheeks flamed at the unladylike observation. Well, at least some of the tension was broken now.

"Antonia!" Rosamond gasped, while Denholm's eyes strayed toward her afflicted anatomy. "Sit down, miss," Lady Thirkell hissed. "I could care less for the condition of your posterior. I will not have it appear that we've been routed."

The actors were taking their third curtain call, and a few patrons were leaving to avoid the crush when a voice from the pit cried "Author!" It was echoed by another, then by others, till the gallery took up the chant and soon the entire theater joined in to swell the cry to thunderous proportions.

Antonia, who had thought that nothing could possibly be more horrifying than the discovery that Denholm's life was being made public upon the stage, soon found herself looking back upon that period of the evening as an oasis of tranquillity. For now the beautiful lady in black whom she'd admired and remarked upon earlier in the evening was rising to her feet and graciously nodding in response to the wild cheering. And then, slowly, deliberately, she turned their way, and, as all eyes followed her lovely gaze, she bent a smile, more enigmatic than *La Gioconda*'s, upon the shuttered face of the Honorable Fitzhugh Denholm.

Chapter Twelve

Three years earlier, Lord Byron had awakened to find himself famous. Now he was being temporarily replaced by a new romantic hero, Fitzhugh Denholm.

Whereas Society originally had sipped its scandal broth while rehashing the more lurid aspects of Denholm's notorious affair, now the teacups clinked to a different tune. To know all, it seemed, was to forgive all. Denholm and Eugenia Lytton Hastings had been elevated to martyrs, their grand passion the victim of selfless duty upon her part and upon his, overweening pride. The ton flocked in droves to see the afterpiece at Drury Lane and, their appetites whetted by the drama portrayed on stage, watched with bated breath for the real-life final act. For had not the Honorable Fitzhugh Denholm returned to London? And was not the beautiful Lady Hastings now free? How long could even a Denholm's pride (though that family was noted for an inordinate amount of that commodity) prevent the course of true love from eventually running smooth? Society eagerly awaited the happy ending.

And Miss Rosamond Thorpe found her position even more intolerable. "Surely Denholm won't offer for me now, will he, Tonia?" she said over the cousins' own cups of tea, taken in Antonia's bedchamber a few mornings after their Drury Lane adventure.

"Why ever not? Nothing has really changed, has it?"

She wrinkled her nose distastefully. "Except for the fact that odious play has brought all the old scandal back to life."

"But that's just the point, don't you see? Everyone's saying that the only reason Lady Hastings agreed to bare her soul on stage was to present her case to Mr. Denholm. They say he had always believed she left him for the Hastings fortune and title. And you know how much false pride he has."

"I know he's proud. I've no way of judging its justification."

"Why, pride's a deadly sin," Rosamond pronounced virtuously. "Didn't they teach you that abroad? But never mind. The point is, Denholm didn't know why she *had* to leave him. How she was duty-bound to the man she had married when he was ill and needed her. And Lord Hastings loved her at least as much as Denholm did. I found his character heartrending, didn't you?"

"I suppose so. I also found Richard the Third villainous, but I did not forget for a minute that Shakespeare made him up."

"Good heavens, Tonia, didn't they teach you anything in school? There actually was a King Richard the Third. And Lord Roderick in the play was actually Lord Hastings. His character was real."

"If you say so. But I didn't see all that much resemblance between the play's hero and the real Mr. Denholm, did you?"

"Well, the actor did seem a great deal nicer." Rosamond sounded regretful. "Though the real Denholm's better-looking," she added with a strange loyalty.

"I can only hope that the real Denholm didn't keep sighing like one of Trevithick's new steam engines starting up. And, frankly, I can't imagine him mouthing all those ridiculous periods that actor kept uttering."

"But then, you weren't there when he was making love,

103

were you? And do you have the slightest notion how a man in love might act?''

Antonia had to admit that she did not, and with that Rosamond steered the conversation back to the phase of the subject foremost on her mind.

"Oh, Tonia, what shall I do if—when—Denholm offers for me? I know people are saying that he will not, that now he knows just how true and noble Lady Hastings really is, they're bound to fall into each other's arms sooner or later. But the thing is,'' she explained as her pretty face grew more troubled, "the ones who are saying that have never met Lord Worth. Oh, Tonia, Denholm's father is the sternest man. He quite frightens me to death. And I don't care how touchingly romantic Mr. Denholm's elopement with Lady Hastings may now appear to the rest of the world, there's no use thinking Lord Worth will ever approve. For she was a married lady. And they did—well, you know—commit adultery—practically beneath the nose of her second husband. Well, he wasn't actually her husband, as it turned out, but that would have nothing to say to Lord Worth's attitude.'' She shuddered.

"Yes, but if, as they're saying, this is the greatest romance since Antony and Cleopatra, I'd hardly think Denholm would let his father's approval or disapproval stand in his way. It certainly didn't when he eloped in the first place. Really, Rosamond, I don't think you need worry.''

"No?'' The other looked unconvinced. "Don't forget, there's always his pride. That could be a bigger obstacle than his father. And if he does offer for me, Tonia, I'll know it's only because of the one or the other. And I don't think I can bear it. It was bad enough to contemplate marrying Mr. Denholm when my deep regard for Cecil and my abhorrence of the life Denholm had lived were the only obstacles. But now that I know he will be pining for another woman during every waking moment of our married lives . . . Oh, Antonia, I don't think I shall be able to bear it!''

104

Though Rosamond's romantic view of the protagonists in *All for Love* prevailed, there was a bit of minority dissent. For one thing, a scathing caricature caused tittering crowds to gather before a particular print shop window. There a drawing portrayed Lady Hastings, in Grecian costume, her beautiful countenance recognizable but avaricious to the point of repulsiveness, furiously writing upon a scroll, while her muse, who bore a strong resemblance to Mr. Burnside, whispered in her ear. Pots of money were stacked at the playwright's feet while Mr. Denholm and Lord Lytton, stripped to their smallclothes, cowered in the corner. Such a twisted version of the great romance of the day was ascribed to the acerbic Mr. Cruikshank. But since the drawing lacked a signature, this was the merest speculation.

Also, Lady Thirkell held the opinion that whether or not Denholm had ever been as besotted by that creature as the drama had portrayed him, no man could stand being placed on exhibition that way. Lady Hastings obviously had no shame. Tying one's garters in public couldn't touch it.

But as to how Denholm himself felt, those supposedly nearest to him could only surmise. For whatever reason, and for several days, he did not put in an appearance either at Wimpole Street or Grosvenor Square. Captain Crosland, a frequent morning caller to both establishments, was able to report, however, that Mr. Denholm, far from having gone into hiding, was very much upon the town. And Antonia and Rosamond were able to verify the truth of this assertion when, promenading in the park accompanied by the faithful captain, they were passed by Mr. Denholm's curricle drawn by a high-stepping pair. He was far too engrossed by the beauty seated on the leather seat beside him to notice them. But they had ample time to ogle him and correct their first impression that the vision beside him was Lady Hastings, a revision made simple by the fact her hair was golden to the point of improbability.

"My word, it's Venus Sheraton!" the captain blurted out, then wished he hadn't, from his expression.

"Oh?" Rosamond turned her troubled gaze upon him. "Who exactly is Miss Sheraton? I don't think I've ever heard of her."

"Oh, no one in particular." He looked uncomfortable. "She's a cyprian, Rosamond."

The captain was disconcerted by Antonia's plainspeaking. Rosamond was shocked. But Antonia herself was less disturbed by the kind of company Mr. Denholm kept than by the fact that his ladybird was wearing her gypsy bonnet.

She was unusually subdued and thoughtful when she returned to Grosvenor Square to find a letter from her father waiting there. After reading it, Antonia abandoned any concern she may or may not have been feeling for Mr. Denholm's tangled affairs. He, she felt sure, would be able to sort out his own life. She would now have to face an issue she'd been avoiding—what to do about her own.

This problem occupied her thoughts for several days. In fact, she was so busy concocting various impractical schemes for her future that, as she crossed St. James's Square after an errand to the linen drapers, she failed to take note of a sporting rig that clattered past her and then suddenly pulled up. The driver had to address her twice. "Where's your abigail?" Mr. Denholm inquired when he'd finally gotten her attention. "You've no business out on the street alone."

"Why ever not? Will someone take me for a lightskirt? But I no longer have the gypsy bonnet."

"You saw that, did you?" Denholm was climbing down from a gleaming high-perch phaeton. "I wondered afterward if that was you we passed. Come on. I'll drive you home."

She thought of three reasons why she should not do so, then succumbed to the lure of the elegant equipage. "This is new, isn't it?" she asked after he'd helped her up and then retrieved the reins.

"Brand-new. Had a run of luck at faro."

Antonia sighed. "I must say, you do seem to contradict everything I was ever taught about the fruits of wickedness."

He laughed. "Don't you believe it. I've been known to pay dearly for my sins. Want to try this out? I was just going to the park."

"Oh, yes." She suppressed a brief vision of what her grandmother might say with the comforting thought that Mrs. Blakeney need never know. For who would be in Hyde Park to see them at this hour? So with her conscience subdued and the threat of rain she'd noted earlier giving way to sunshine, she rechecked the strings on her cherry bonnet and relaxed to enjoy the briskness of the air as they tooled along. After a minute or two spent in discussing the various points of his rig and cattle, Denholm inquired, "What were you thinking of so hard back there? I almost ran you down, and you didn't even notice."

Antonia hesitated a moment, then rejected her first impulse to be evasive. She needed to confide in someone. Grandmother and Lady Thirkell were far too involved. And asking advice from Rosamond would be useless. Certainly no one could be more detached and objective than her companion. "To be honest," she blurted out as he slowed the horses and turned into the entrance to the park, "I was trying to form some acceptable scheme for my future."

"Oh?" An eyebrow lifted underneath his jauntily cocked beaver. "Forgive my denseness, but what 'acceptable scheme' can there possibly be other than marriage?"

"Well, I'd always supposed that after my visit here, I would rejoin Papa and keep house for him."

"And now?"

"He's getting married."

"I see. That does upset things. Do you know the lady?"

"Yes." She did not quite succeed in sounding noncommittal.

"And you don't deal well together?"

"I cannot imagine that we ever could. Besides, Papa has made it clear that I'm not wanted." The hurt in her voice earned a look of sympathy that she missed. "Do you remember when you thought I was Rosamond?"

"How could I forget?" he observed while skillfully maneuvering round a barouche.

"Then, you may recall that whereas at first I thought you'd escaped somehow from your strait jacket, then I was ready to accept the possibility that Papa could have arranged my marriage behind my back. He was so eager to ship me off to England, you see. Now I know that it was his own he wished to arrange." She unleashed her bitterness. "And he urges me to make the most of my opportunities here. He doesn't even mind that I'm with Grandmother, though he's kept her secret from me all my life. The important thing is that I have Lady Thirkell's patronage. I tell you, I have never been so disillusioned. Why, there's not a penny's worth of difference between Uncle Edwin and my papa. He's practically ordering me to cast myself upon the marriage mart."

"I don't wish to appear as hopelessly crass as your relatives, but isn't that the fate of every young lady of our class? And haven't you, in effect, already done just that—entered the marriage mart, I mean? This is, after all, the purpose of a come-out."

"Well, *I* did not consider it so. I only thought of it as an interlude, an adventure, if you will, before I took up my old life again."

"Where you eventually would have married."

"Not necessarily. At least, I would not have felt forced to do so. And Papa is saying that he is absolutely opposed to my marrying a soldier. And that I must take advantage of my opportunities here in London."

"Well, why not? I've never noticed any scarcity of young bucks dangling after you."

"Dangling, yes. But if you think one of them is going to come up to scratch and offer for a girl without a fortune, well, you certainly are a disappointment. Everyone's always saying how worldly you are. And if you think that, well, you're a green 'un.''

"It's been known to happen. Remember the penniless Gunning sisters? They married peers. Right down to the final Gunning.''

"There were only two of them, not a bevy. They were also nonpareils.''

"I'll let that pass. I can't stand females who dangle after compliments.''

"And I can't stand males who feel compelled to talk flattering fustian. I am serious.''

"Yes, I can see that.''

"And the thing is, even if I were a Gunning, I have yet to see a man I'd wish to marry. And I cannot go on indefinitely sponging off Lady Thirkell.''

"I wouldn't worry about that too much. Aunt Kate can well afford it.''

"But I've no claim upon her. It's enough that she supports Grandmother, which I long to do. I'd even dreamed of taking her back to Belgium. For what's to happen to her if Lady Thirkell dies?''

"You really are blue-deviled. I'm quite confident that Aunt Kate will have provided for her. Want me to ask her?''

"No! That would never do. Oh, would you? I mean, not directly. But could you hint? For if I knew that Grandmother was provided for, well, then, I could feel much freer about seeking a post for myself.''

"What kind of post?'' he asked as he whipped up his team. "Can you do anything?''

"Well . . .'' She sounded doubtful. "I could be a governess to very small children, I suppose. Before they needed to be taught much more than their ABCs.''

"I doubt there's much demand for that,'' he observed dampeningly.

"You're probably right. I should perhaps be a companion."

"And become a dogsbody? Believe me, the relationship between Aunt Kate and your grandmother is hardly typical. You'd hate it. Your father's right. You'd better marry."

She glared. "You haven't paid the slightest attention to what I've said, have you? I've just explained why I cannot."

He narrowed his eyes to study the gait of the leftside horse. "Would you like for me to offer for you? Again."

"I don't find that amusing. I know I've no right to dump my troubles upon you, but you did ask and could at least take me seriously. And I had thought it just possible, considering all you yourself have been through, that you might be a bit more understanding than the average, though why I should have thought so defies all reason. I collect I must have let that ridiculous play influence me. I should have remembered that that sensitive, caring man on stage was not really you."

"You're damned right he wasn't," Denholm snapped. "And if you'll climb down off your high ropes a minute, we—"

Whatever he had intended to say was interrupted by a horseman cantering past in the opposite direction. The rider abruptly reined in and shouted after them, "Fitz! Fitzhugh Denholm! Is that really you, or has your ghost come back to haunt me?"

Mr. Denholm abruptly pulled up his team, thrust the reins into Antonia's hands, and leaped down from the phaeton. "I won't be a minute," he called over his shoulder as he went to join the friend who was tactfully waiting at a little distance in case he did not wish to introduce his female companion. With a great deal of back-thumping and shoulder-slapping, each man explained to the other how he happened to be back in England and then arranged a more lengthy reunion for later on that evening. When Denholm

110

returned to his rig five minutes later, he found that Antonia had moved over into his place.

"Could I please drive?"

"No. Scoot over."

"But I'd give anything to learn. Ladies do, you know. I saw two driving in the park just the other day."

"In a high-perch phaeton?"

"Yes. And the woman driving seemed a perfect hand."

"No doubt. But I daresay she didn't learn on that particular rig. Perhaps I'll let you drive my curricle someday."

"Driving a phaeton doesn't look so difficult."

"It is. Besides, I wish to finish our conversation, not wind up in the ditch."

"Our conversation is already finished as far as I'm concerned." She was reluctantly scooting across the leather seat to avoid being sat upon. "And, as for ditches, I've no intention of—oh, dear, my reticule." She had somehow swept her purse off the other side.

Sighing, Denholm dismounted again and walked round the rear of the phaeton to retrieve it. Then, just as he bent to do so, Miss Thorpe gave the reins a glorious snap and sprang the horses. He watched, cursing beneath his breath, while his team and its female driver galloped out of sight.

At first Antonia felt only exhilaration as the perfectly matched grays sped down the carriage road. It was the curricle race all over again, made even more exciting by her elevated perch and sense of power. Her bonnet was blown back off her curls, but this time the ribbons held and it bounced merrily against her back while the wind played havoc with the Grecian arrangement of her hair. Since the team showed a decided preference for keeping to the center of the road, it was most fortunate that the traffic was quite light. It was only when she tried to pull her horses to one side to avoid a landau that Antonia realized she might be in a bit of trouble. The pair refused to yield an inch. The coachman of the oncoming carriage headed for the open

111

field while the lady passengers squealed and their escorts hurled oaths at the flying phaeton.

"So, I'm not yet quite ready for the Whip Club," she told herself aloud; "driving is famous!" Although she now recognized some of her inadequacy, it never occurred to her that she'd be unable to stop whenever she desired till she pulled hard upon the reins and shouted "Whoa!" and the pace accelerated. And as if this were not sufficient warning, the full import of her predicament was now brought home by the shocked expression of a horseman who had just roweled his steed to avoid her. "Help! Runaways!" Antonia screeched as she sped on by him.

Captain Crosland acted with all the courage, daring, and dispatch that had made England victor over the upstart Napoleon. He wheeled his horse and tore off in hot pursuit, overtaking the runaway rig and managing to grab hold of the harness and slow the horses down to a gradual halt. "Are you all right, Miss Thorpe?" he asked solicitously, noting her chalk-white face.

"C-certainly." Antonia did not protest, however, when Captain Crosland secured his horse to the rear of the phaeton and took the reins from her nerveless fingers. But she did recover sufficiently to give an edited explanation of her circumstance before they rounded the curve to the scene of her piracy. The captain heard her out, chuckled, and agreed to trade places with her, adding there was little danger of a repeat performance since the horses were now run quite off their feet.

Denholm, leaning against a tree and scowling, was thereupon treated to the sight of Miss Thorpe, her bonnet sedately in place, who was very much in command of the situation, while Captain Crosland lounged beside her, casually lighting up a brown cheroot. "I've had the most glorious spin," Antonia announced in a bright voice that was almost steady. "And look who I ran into—chanced upon, I mean to say."

Mr. Denholm held his pose while his narrowed eyes

112

traveled from her chalky face, to the flecks of foam upon his team, to Crosland's dishevelment. With a Herculean effort he refrained from comment and merely nodded briefly to the captain as he strolled over to reclaim his rig. He had missed his opportunity, for Miss Thorpe chatted desperately of this and that all the way back to Grosvenor Square, never allowing him or Captain Crosland to slip in so much as a word.

Chapter Thirteen

The Honorable Fitzhugh Denholm was a great deal more knowing than Miss Antonia Thorpe. He was well aware when he was being manipulated. But it suited him to act upon Captain Crosland's casually dropped regrets that he'd spent too much time in the army to gain admission to any of London's exclusive clubs. He invited him to be his guest at Brooks's that very evening. And after several hours of play in the Great Subscription Room, wherein the captain won a modest sum and Denholm fared even better, they settled down with brandy and cigars to the real business of the evening.

Denholm allowed the captain to do his none-too-subtle probing first. And after a few inquiries concerning Miss Antonia Thorpe's status in the Thirkell household and Mr. Denholm's opinion of the rumors that her ladyship might make the girl her heir, when none of the answers proved satisfactory, he turned the conversation around to Miss Rosamond Thorpe.

Here the captain felt his way a bit more carefully. But he wound up with the confirmed impression that Sir Edwin's only child did indeed have great expectations and that, although nothing had been definitely settled yet, the nabob opposite, so casually regarding him through a cloud of smoke, was going to become a rival to Croesus through a marriage to the fair Rosamond. The world was indeed unjust, the captain concluded, when a here-and-thereian like Denholm had it all and a stout fellow like himself was forced to scrape by on his charm and wit.

But when it came to learning what one wished to know, two could play at the same game. Without needing to resort to the kind of digging the other had employed, Mr. Denholm was able to confirm his impression that Captain Crosland was a blatant fortune hunter and would not do for Miss Antonia Thorpe.

There was one thing, though, that had been puzzling Denholm about the soldier, and scorning the other's devious methods, he asked his question bluntly. "How does it happen, Captain, that with Napoleon on the rampage again, you've been able to spend so much time in England?"

"Well, it's not a thing I care to talk about." Crosland assumed an air of proper modesty. "Wounded, you know. Needed a good deal of time to recuperate. Bad timing on my part, of course. Hate to miss such a show." His expression now was downcast, and Denholm noticed as they left the club that his limp, heretofore unnoticeable, had become quite pronounced.

Sleep was slow in coming when the Honorable Fitzhugh Denholm finally blew out his candle in St. James Street. He found his troubled thoughts returning more than once to Miss Antonia Thorpe. What on earth had caused him to be so quixotic as to mention offering for her? Thank God she hadn't taken him seriously. The question he couldn't answer was whether or not he had been. Oh, there was no doubt in his mind that he'd much prefer to be married to her than to her vacuous cousin, but since the only purpose in marrying was to please his long-suffering parents, such a preference had nothing at all to say in the matter. Lord and Lady Worth might prefer Antonia to Eugenia Lytton Hastings, he should say—but only barely. No, that particular alliance was not to be considered.

But he continued to think of Antonia anyhow, in order

115

to avoid more painful thoughts; so he surmised. And he realized that he was quite concerned for her. A step up, he mocked himself, from his usual absorption with his own self-inflicted problems.

He had never before considered the plight of the gently bred young female who had no fortune. Few, if any, in that category had been flung at his head back during the interlude when he'd been considered the biggest catch on the marriage mart, before Eugenia Lytton had tossed her cap over the windmill and run off with him. No, Antonia was right. Money married money. In the main, at least. But there were exceptions. Men did now and again lose their heads over certain women. He—and his smile was bitter there in the darkness—was living proof of that. Antonia Thorpe was hardly a femme fatale, though. Still, she did have a rather unique appeal. His smile changed character as he recalled once more the way she'd cheered him on during their curricle race and the sly way she'd left him eating her dust after she'd made off with his rig that morning. But those particular episodes might not endear her to every man, he realized. Denholm frowned and began to make a mental listing of his eligible friends. He came up with a few who just might be interested in a fortuneless young woman of unusual style. It wouldn't hurt him to take a few coves calling at Grosvenor Square. After that, it was up to Antonia Thorpe to make the most of the opportunities he provided.

Denholm felt quite virtuous after this resolve, and he expected the altruistic decision to help him fall asleep. But the thoughts he'd striven to keep at bay came back to torment him. And once more he watched the jackanapes who had portrayed him cavort upon the stage, and through a red haze of anger he saw the gorgeous, triumphant face of Eugenia smiling her knowing smile. He swore vehemently. Then relighted his candle and picked up his sketchpad.

Miss Antonia Thorpe's own first choice for keeping unwelcome thoughts at bay would have been increased activity. But one could not always be paying or receiving calls, and Lady Thirkell's enormous staff of servants precluded making herself useful around the house. As a consequence, Antonia was a frequent visitor to the circulating libraries.

On one such visit, as she edged her way around the shelves, scanning titles, she felt that she was under surveillance. But when she turned to glance at the few other patrons present, she concluded she was imagining things. No one was looking her way. Nor did she recognize any acquaintance. Antonia returned her attention to the serious business of book selection; still, she could not shake the feeling she was being watched. This time she turned more quickly and spied a soberly dressed young man staring her way.

He reddened and approached her. "Pray forgive my boldness in addressing you, Miss Thorpe. Miss *Rosamond* Thorpe said I might find you here and that, under the circumstances, you would not require that we stand on ceremony."

"Oh, are you Mr. Hollingsworth?" Antonia was unable to conceal her astonishment that this was Rosamond's curate, so little did the pale young man with his pale hair and eyes match the Adonis image Rosamond had painted.

"Might I have a private word with you?" From his nervousness, Mr. Cecil Hollingsworth appeared to consider this a most improper suggestion.

"Why, of course." Antonia smiled to set him at ease and, indicating an unoccupied table, went to take a seat. There was a slight delay before the curate followed and sat across from her. He had deemed it necessary to bring along a book as subterfuge and chose to whisper at her across its open pages.

"Miss Rosamond Thorpe tells me that she has made you her confidante." He blushed above the plain white stock he wore.

"Why, y-yes." Antonia's hesitation was not due to con-

117

tracted nervousness, but to the fact that it had been so long since the curate's name had cropped up in her cousin's conversation, she had almost forgot those early transports. Now she looked expectantly at the young man, waiting for him to come to the point.

But his pulpit training did not permit such directness. He built up slowly to a climax, dwelling at whispered length upon the high regard in which Miss Rosamond held her cousin and the admiration that she accorded the other's ability to take decisive action. "Miss Rosamond Thorpe herself would have never been able to slip away from the Hall and embark for London on the public stage as you did. Nor would I wish her to." In fact, Mr. Hollingsworth could hardly hide his horror at the notion. "But while as a man of the cloth I cannot approve of such a drastic course for any gently bred young lady," he felt obliged to say, "I must at the same time acknowledge the degree of courage such an action showed."

Antonia was about to protest that there was nothing particularly heroic about boarding a coach when the curate forged ahead. "And I must also add that as much as I naturally abhor flouting parental authority, I can see how in Sir Edwin's case you were goaded to do so. He is not an easy man to deal with."

Antonia did wish the prosy young man would not find it necessary to absolve her character before coming to the point. "Why did my cousin wish you to speak to me?" she asked.

He looked a bit offended at such directness. "Rosamond—Miss Thorpe, I should say—feels that anyone as resourceful as you is sure to find a way around our difficulties."

"And just what specific difficulty did she have in mind?"

"Why, in the first place, how to save Rosamond from being sold to that—that—devil's disciple!"

"Mr. Denholm?"

"Of course Mr. Denholm." The curate was beginning

118

to think that his beloved's faith in her cousin's acumen was misplaced. "You are aware of Sir Edwin's ambitions in that regard, are you not, Miss Thorpe?"

"Oh, yes. Of course. Certainly. I'd just never heard Mr. Denholm described in quite those terms before."

"Pray forgive my lack of delicacy. I should not perhaps have done so. But when I think of my sweet, pure Rosamond bartered to such a man, I am beside myself."

"Well, yes, I can see that," Antonia said hastily. His voice had risen from a whisper to an impassioned squeak, and heads were turning toward them. "I do sympathize with your position, Mr. Hollingsworth, but I really don't see what I can do about it."

The curate was looking more and more disillusioned. "We had hoped you could persuade your uncle to see reason. Mr. Denholm can only make dear Rosamond miserable. I could make her happy."

"Well, yes, I suppose so." Antonia had not intended to sound so doubtful on the second score. "But the thing is, as you've just noted, Uncle Edwin and I do not deal well together."

"Ah, yes." As a man of the cloth Mr. Hollingsworth was probably not in the habit of playing aces, but his tone of voice would have been appropriate for such a contingency. "But you have a most formidable ally—Lady Thirkell. It is Rosamond's impression that her ladyship does not wish Mr. Denholm to marry her. If this is so, could you not persuade her to make her desires known? Sir Edwin, according to Rosamond, stands in great awe of her."

"*Everyone* stands in great awe of Lady Thirkell," Antonia retorted. "Including me. And I can hardly see myself persuading her of anything."

"Well, I must say that Rosamond will be very disappointed." The curate was decidedly huffy by now. "She relied on you. I don't think it even occurred to her that you would be so unsympathetic."

"I'm not unsympathetic," Antonia was stung into declaring. "It's just that I feel it would be an abuse of her ladyship's hospitality for me to meddle in her family affairs." What she didn't confide to the curate was that she feared her ladyship might find her motives suspect. She had awakened to the fact that Lady Thirkell was developing an alarming tendency to throw her at Mr. Denholm's head. "No, it would be quite improper for me to try to influence her ladyship. And I've no chance whatsoever in changing Uncle's mind." She raised a hand to cut off whatever new reproaches were forming on the curate's lips. "But I will promise to think on the problem very seriously." She rose to her feet dismissively. "And then I'll discuss the matter with Rosamond." Since the curate's expression suggested a prisoner denied his stay of execution, Antonia was moved to add, "Come now, cheer up, Mr. Hollingsworth. Things cannot be as black as they now appear. Love will always find a way."

Antonia could not believe that such a preposterous bromide had actually emerged from her own mouth. Was it perhaps a line from *All for Love*? It certainly rang as false as the rest of that cloying drama. She glanced at Mr. Hollingsworth, braced for a scathing setdown.

The clergyman, however, was looking at her with new respect. His pale eyes glowed. There could be no doubt about it. Mr. Hollingsworth was most definitely heartened.

Chapter Fourteen

Mrs. Blakeney thoroughly approved of Captain Crosland. He was everything she desired in a grandson—handsome, charming, attentive to old ladies. She had decided that he would be perfect for Antonia. After all, they came from the same background, he knew of her straitened circumstances, and he obviously had private means. The fact that he was on such easy terms with so many of the ton suggested at least a competency, if not actual wealth. He had just been entertaining Antonia and several morning callers with a lively account of an evening at his exclusive club. When the others had left and the captain was still there, the scheming Mrs. Blakeney contrived to leave him and her granddaughter alone together.

Well, not literally alone or it would have been much too improper to excuse herself to tend to a domestic matter. Lady Thirkell was with them, ensconced in her favorite wing chair, her feet resting on a painted cross-framed stool. But her ladyship had been receiving visitors for the better part of two hours, and her head was beginning to nod. Mrs. Blakeney was sure that in a few moments' time the attractive young couple would be entirely private, a state of affairs she knew the captain yearned for.

Her deduction proved correct. As Captain Crosland prosed on at length about the play in Brooks's Subscription Room, his narrative was soon punctuated with snores. He broke it off. "Miss Rosamond has made me her confidant," he said, being careful not to change his tone of voice.

"I beg your pardon?" Antonia had not been attending. In fact, she had almost followed their hostess's example. "Confided about what, I mean to say," she rallied.

"About the monstrous coil she's in—forced into a marriage she finds abhorrent while her heart belongs to another."

"Oh, yes, that. Of course." If Antonia was a bit surprised that her shy cousin had been so open, she thought it impolite to say so.

"And she tells me that you mean to help. I think that's splendid of you."

"Well . . ." She glanced at Lady Thirkell, whose chin was now resting on her collarbone. "Yes, I have said that I would try. And, to tell the truth, I've thought of little else. But I don't really see how. Uncle Edwin has his heart set on this match, you know."

"Yes, I do know." Captain Crosland leaned toward her and lowered his voice. "And I agree with you. On the surface, matching Miss Rosamond with the man of her choice seems hopeless. We need to approach the problem from another angle."

Antonia did not miss the "we." But she was no further enlightened and said so.

"Really, Miss Thorpe, it's very simple. We must see to it that Mr. Denholm weds someone else."

"Perhaps you think that's simple. But I certainly don't see how we,"—she stressed the pronoun—"can possibly do anything of the kind."

"Merely by providing the opportunity. After all, Denholm already loves another. He is, in fact, the victim of a grand passion that makes Miss Thorpe and her curate—pray do not repeat this to your cousin—seem like two young mooncalves."

"Oh? And has Mr. Denholm also confided in you?"

"Not in so many words." His knowing look implied an understanding between gentlemen. "But you were in Drury Lane. At Miss Rosamond's insistence I went myself the other night. Can you doubt the depth of the attachment?"

"Well, no, I suppose not."

Antonia had no desire to pursue that subject any further, but the captain seemed unaware of her reluctance. "It's obviously only pride that stands in the way. Lady Hastings tells me that is the major obstacle to their happiness, the thing that makes Denholm determined to keep avoiding her."

"You know Lady Hastings!"

"Shhh!" In her astonishment Antonia had allowed her voice to rise. Lady Thirkell raised her head, looked all around the withdrawing room, then nodded off once more. "Yes. After my conversation with Miss Rosamond I took it upon myself to gain an introduction to Lady Hastings in order to discuss your cousin's situation. And I must say her ladyship's gratitude for my doing so was most touching. She had heard rumors of an understanding between Denholm and Miss Rosamond and is convinced that such a match could only cause great unhappiness to the parties most concerned. She's quite sure of Denholm's love, you see." He broke into his train of thought to ask, "Have you ever seen Lady Hastings?"

"Yes. From a distance."

"Then, you can well imagine that any man could easily fall under her spell. And one who, like Denholm, has been on such intimate terms with her ladyship—pray forgive my candor—could not easily free himself from that spell. If it were not for his fierce pride and all-consuming jealousy—"

"You must forgive me, Captain Crosland," Antonia interrupted rather rudely. She was finding this conversation more and more distasteful. "But I really don't see what all this has to do with me."

"That's what I'm trying to explain." He frowned. "To put it simply, we must find a way to bring those two parted lovers back together. And since you seem to have considerable influence with Denholm—"

"That's ridiculous," she protested. "I've no such thing."

But as if to disprove her words, Morton appeared at that moment to announce, "Lord Thayer Edgemon and Mr. Denholm, your ladyship."

"Oh, there you are, Fitzhugh." Lady Thirkell snapped to, adjusted her cap, which had slipped down upon her forehead, and fastened her wide-awake gaze upon her nephew. "Thought you'd probably gone into hiding after that odious woman's odious play. Glad to see you ain't. Best to outface the gossipmongers, I always say."

"What I like most about you, Aunt Kate, is your remarkable tact and delicacy." Mr. Denholm, looking unusually elegant in a blue tailcoat with brass buttons worn over a fawn waistcoat, nodded at the others and strolled over to kiss her cheek. "You remember my friend Thayer, of course."

Lord Thayer, despite his tailor's efforts to minimize his slightly rotund figure with dark-blue superfine worn with gray, still fell far below his friend's sartorial splendor. Under the old lady's stare, he turned pink and bowed.

"Of course. Couldn't forget him, more's the pity. Helped you liberate me parrot. Nasty little boys, both of you. Antonia, ring for more tea. Oh, never mind, here it is." The butler had made a reappearance. "But you don't know my companion's granddaughter, now, do you? Antonia, this is Lord Thayer Edgemon. Thayer, Miss Antonia Thorpe. And the military gentleman is Captain Crosland."

His lordship murmured a polite acknowledgment to both introductions, but his amiable face had grown bemused. Antonia was feeling most uncomfortable, whereas the captain found the situation intriguing until he realized her ladyship was looking pointedly at him as she poured out only four cups of tea and was reminded that he had flagrantly overstayed the prescribed twenty minutes for morning calls.

After the captain's departure, Lord Thayer returned his puzzled gaze to Antonia and inquired politely. "Ain't we met before, Miss Thorpe? Nearly sure of it."

"I pointed Miss Thorpe out to you when we were out riding," Denholm offered, and suppressed a smile as the light finally dawned upon his friend.

"Oh, *that's* who you are. Didn't realize. What I mean to say is, you don't look the same. That is, I didn't expect to find you here. Couldn't have, of course, just having seen you riding in the park that way," he finished lamely.

"And speaking of driving," Denholm chimed in none too subtly, while taking a proffered cup from his aunt's hand, "Miss Thorpe here has expressed a burning desire to learn to drive a curricle, Thayer. And since you're so devilish proud of your new equipage and inclined to show off at every opportunity, it occurred to me that you are the very one to teach her. I assure you, Miss Thorpe, no one's more qualified than his lordship to be your instructor. His prowess as a whip is legendary."

"Oh, I say," Lord Thayer protested.

"Really, Mr. Denholm." Antonia glared.

"Nonsense!" Lady Thirkell thundered, and got the floor. "What's the meaning of this, Antonia?"

"Miss Thorpe wishes to learn to drive, ma'am." Denholm forestalled whatever answer Antonia might have made. "More and more young ladies are doing so. It's quite the thing, in fact. I hope you've no objection."

"I've no objection to Antonia learning. Think it's a capital notion, in fact. Been thinking of getting a sporting rig. She can drive me. What I object to is having Thayer teach her. Now, no need to look offended," she said soothingly to her titled guest, "I'm sure you're a dab hand, boy. But me nevvy's coming it too strong when he says no one's more qualified to teach Antonia. Pack of nonsense. He is."

"Thank you for your vote of confidence, Aunt Kate. But the thing is, it will not be convenient for me to teach Miss

Thorpe." He gave his relative a speaking look that was entirely wasted.

Denholm had been rather proud of this scheme to bring Lord Thayer and Miss Thorpe together. Thayer had no need to marry money. He was also painfully shy where the ladies were concerned. Driving was his greatest passion. Denholm, therefore, had counted on Miss Thorpe's own enthusiasm for that sport to break down Thayer's bashfulness and give them a common interest to counteract his usual tongue-tied state. Trust Aunt Kate to blow the gaff!

"Well, then, it's settled," that autocrat pronounced. "You'll teach Antonia to drive, Fitzhugh. Call for her at nine tomorrow."

"No, Aunt."

"Too early, eh? Humph. Planning to be on the town all night, I collect. Oh, very well. Make it nine-thirty, then. No later. Won't do to let the traffic get too heavy."

"What won't do, Aunt Kate, is for me to teach Miss Thorpe to drive." Denholm's exasperation was evident. Antonia's initial annoyance had turned to amusement. She took a quick sip of tea to cover up her smile. "To be as blunt as you are wont to be, dear relative, have you forgotten my reputation? Surely you don't wish to make Miss Thorpe grist for the gossipmongers' mill?"

"She won't be," Lady Thirkell said complacently. "Nothing could be more natural than for you two to be seen together. Everyone knows that Antonia is my ward and you are my heir."

"I didn't know it!" Lord Thayer Edgemon blurted out, as Antonia strangled on her tea. "Never knew either one of those things. The ward business don't surprise me. But hadn't the slightest notion you were her ladyship's heir, Fitz."

"No, I expect you didn't, for it isn't true. Any more than it's true that Tonia—Miss Thorpe—is her ward. My aunt will stop at nothing, including the most out-and-out rappers, to get her own way."

126

"Oh, very well." The old lady looked sheepish. "You've caught me out. But the true or false of the thing don't signify. Your concern was with what people will say when they see you two out driving together at nine-thirty A.M. sharp. And that's what they'll say. Or would if they saw you, which they won't, for no self-respecting member of the ton will be in Hyde Park at such an ungodly hour.

"Now do run along, Fitzhugh, and take Thayer with you. For I need me nap. And Mrs. Blakeney is the only person I know of who actually would be shocked if I left her granddaughter alone with a man of your reputation. By the by, Antonia, no need to mention this driving business to her. Shouldn't say so, for she's me dearest friend, but your grandmama's too strait-laced by half. I tell you, there's nothing like leading a scandalous life to turn an otherwise normal person into a pattern card of virtue."

Chapter Fifteen

"How does it feel to have been hoist by your own petard?" Antonia inquired as they turned into Hyde Park. The morning was chill and damp with fog, making her envy Denholm's five-caped greatcoat, more suitable to the capricious weather than the light pelisse she wore. Hers were the first words spoken since a perfunctory greeting when he'd arrived at Grosvenor Square promptly at nine-thirty. Antonia had been ready and waiting but had not actually expected him to appear. Since she deduced from his haggard face he'd been up for most of the night, his presence was a tribute to Lady Thirkell's forcefulness. Even a confirmed rebel didn't dare to cross her.

"Just what petard was that?"

"Oh, don't play the innocent. I'm well aware you've been flinging suitors at my head ever since I told you of my father's marriage plans. And I suppose that kind of reaction to my Cheltenham tragedy serves me right. And I'll even go so far as to suppose that you mean well by it. But I find it all rather humiliating. Poor Lord Thayer! He was quite ready to sink. As for me, I've learned my lesson. I'll never tie my garters in public again. So, pray try to forget that I ever confided in you."

"I've been wondering about that." He pulled his team to a halt and turned to look at her. "Why did you?"

"I've asked myself the same question," she replied candidly. "And the truth is, I haven't the slightest idea. You were there, of course."

"That's certainly one requirement of a confidant."

"But I suppose the main thing was that it was perfectly safe to do so. Or at least I thought so."

"Safe?"

"Well, for one thing, you weren't likely to overset me by being too sympathetic, as my grandmother might have done."

"Thank you."

"And you certainly give the impression that anything told you would be treated with all the sanctity of the confessional. You are probably the most private person I've ever met."

"*Private,* Miss Thorpe?" His lip curled. "You'd best consult Mr. Johnson's dictionary. I am in fact the most *public* person you'll likely meet. How many others of your acquaintance can boast of having the most intimate details of their lives dramatized on stage?"

"But that's exactly what I mean. It's bound to have been simply awful for you. But you don't betray your feelings. And so, I had believed that you'd respect my—outpourings—and not betray them."

"Surely you don't think I did?" he protested. "I can assure you—"

"Oh, I know you haven't gossiped about me. But what you have done is almost worse. For you were the last person I should have expected to turn matchmaker. There is one thing you need to understand, Mr. Denholm. You do not have an exclusive claim to pride. I have my share as well. And I find it humiliating to become an object of your charity."

"Charity!" The word became an epithet. "Is that what you think? Well, you're quite wrong, Miss Thorpe. But your point is well taken, nonetheless. In the future I shall remind myself to mind my own business—which at the moment, God help me, is to teach you to drive. So, let's get on with it.'' He then imprudently leaped down from the driver's seat and winced when the impact jarred his aching head.

"Shot the cat last night, did you?'' Antonia observed without much sympathy as she scooted into the driver's seat. "Well, I did not intend to put you into such a taking.''

"A taking? Me?'' He climbed up beside her. "Whatever gave you such a maggoty notion? I'm the man who never shows his feelings, so you just said. Those, Miss Thorpe, are the reins. Now pick them up.''

The lesson proceeded in near silence except for the necessary instructions succinctly delivered and promptly acted upon. Antonia, who was beginning to regret so much plain-speaking, devoted herself to being as apt a pupil as was possible. And from her own point of view she succeeded so well that she soon forgot all else but the joy of handling such a superb team hitched to the smoothest running rig it had ever been her privilege to ride in.

So pleased was she with her progress, in fact, that when a foppish young man in a natty bright red curricle pulled alongside intending to pass them, she gave him an impish grin and whipped up her horses. The young man gleefully accepted the challenge and urged his own team on.

"What the devil! Have you lost your mind?'' Denholm reached for the reins and got his wrist slapped. "God help you, then, if you damage my cattle or so much as scratch this rig,'' he growled. And then with a raw courage that would have done justice to a Spartan, he braced his feet, folded his arms, and let his pupil have her head.

Antonia's enthusiasm proved contagious. Denholm's detached disapproval lasted all of thirty seconds before he fell victim to her sparkling eyes and delighted laughter as they pulled a few paces ahead of the red curricle on the tree-lined avenue. He grinned back at her and began to issue rapid instructions.

On the straightaway there was no contest. The superiority of the Denholm cattle compensated for Antonia's inexperience. But when the road curved sharply, the tutor felt it time to intervene. He put his arms around the driver, his gloved hands closed above her own and reined the horses in. The red rig swept around them with a triumphant shout.

"Oh, how could you be so craven? We could have won. Easily."

Denholm was about to retort that what they could have done was land the curricle in a ditch with themselves hurled God knows where, when he suddenly abandoned the whole idea of explanation. Antonia's lips were entirely too near for such reasonableness. He kissed them. And met a response so intense that it took his breath away and destroyed the last vestiges of his common sense.

There was a sweet desperation in Antonia's kiss. For while her emotions were acknowledging the truth her mind had sought to hide, her intelligence still operated enough for her to know that this was all she could ever expect from such a misguided attachment, and she should do her best to make a memory good enough to last.

After their first widened start of surprise her eyes had closed, her fingers had sent his beaver toppling to entangle with his hair, and she had simply surrendered to the wonderful, heavy glow that overpowered her. She would never have dreamed that the mere touch of lips, the teasing of tongues, could turn the balance of nature topsy-turvy, bringing stars out in midmorning to spiral and cavort and calling the larks home early from their winter quarters to warble a serenade. All she really knew was that she wanted the moment to last forever—and for this man to love her.

Both notions were ridiculous, of course. As Fitzhugh Denholm soon demonstrated. Though it did seem to take considerable effort to disengage himself, he managed. And his rather dazed expression as he gazed into her equally bemused eyes quickly turned to self-reproach. "I knew it was sheer insanity for me to teach you to drive," he said huskily.

"Well, no need to reproach yourself." Her smile was forced. She'd been wrong when she'd spoken of his skill at hiding what he felt. Emotion was written large upon his face. And of all the things he might have been feeling at the moment, the revealed reaction was the one she wished for least: he seemed completely overcome with guilt.

"I do reproach myself. My God, you're just a child. You probably think by now that every curricle race ends in a kiss. That it's part of the ritual."

"Like cutting off the fox's brush at the end of a hunt? Don't be absurd."

"Don't joke. I'm trying to be serious. The point is, Tonia, I came back to England thinking I could straighten out my life. Well, I was wrong. It's in a bigger mess than ever. There's my father's matchmaking. Eugenia's theatricals. God knows, all that would be coil enough for any normal man. But what do I do but complicate things further by making love to a schoolroom miss. No, do be quiet for one minute, Antonia. What I'm trying to tell you is that I'm the last man on earth you should be entangled with. But since matters seem to have taken their own turn, let me say—"

A kid glove was clapped none too gently over his mouth. Blue eyes glared. "Denholm, don't you dare offer for me again. It will be the third time, and I call that the outside of enough. No wonder you ran off to the Continent. If your conscience can goad you into proposing marriage over a simple—well, let's not call it that—over a *complicated* kiss that no one knows of but us, I can well see why, under those circumstances, you felt you had to elope. No, do be quiet! The only thing you've said so far that makes any sense is that your life is in disarray and you shouldn't make things worse. Do you know what I think?"

"No, but I'm sure you're about to tell me."

"I think you should declare a moratorium on offering

132

anything to any woman—marrige, elopement, carte blanche, whatever. For at least a year. Till you can learn to overcome your odd bent toward chivalry. Really, Denholm, your reputation as a rake seems undeserved. You haven't the slightest notion of how a scoundrel operates. Good heavens, even I—schoolroom miss or not—know that no one gets compromised by a mere kiss. You act as though you'd made me *enceinte*." She punctuated this shocking remark by skillfully cracking the whip and springing the horses. His arms were around her once more, his hands on the reins.

"Please don't do that again." To her mortification, tears stung her eyes.

"Don't worry" was the grim answer as he tugged the horses to a halt once more. "The only thing I intend to resume is the driving lesson. And here's the final, most important pointer of the day. Never let your emotions affect your driving. A good whip never takes his anger out on his cattle. Now, then. I'd say this has been more than enough instruction for one day. I declare the lesson finished. Scoot over. I'll drive."

He remembered how she'd left him high and dry before, so he took no chances. Instead of climbing down and around, he scrambled across her knees and displaced her none too gently. "A good instructor never takes his anger out on his pupil," she mimicked as he flicked his reins. "By the by, you've lost your hat."

"Blast!" He clapped a glove to his head in confirmation, then set to work smoothing his disheveled locks. "Well, what could I expect? Isn't that a part of the ritual, too, when we ride together? Losing hats. My turn again."

"We could go back and get it," she said practically.

"I've got others. It's more than time to get you home."

They rode in silence, sitting as far apart as the seat allowed, neither glancing back as carriage wheels approached.

"Oh, I say, Denholm!" A male shout behind them

133

caused both to turn. Denholm's response was to increase their speed. Nothing of the previous lesson had been lost on Antonia, though. She reached over, grabbed his hands, and tugged on the reins. "It's Captain Crosland. He's got your hat."

Seconds later, Antonia regretted her impetuosity. Unlike her driver, she'd failed to recognize the captain's passenger. Crosland skillfully guided his phaeton up beside them, placing Mr. Denholm and Lady Hastings close enough to touch.

A close-up view of the famous Eugenia Lytton-Hastings put the final touches on Antonia's rotten day. From a distance the lady had seemed merely beautiful. Nearby, she took one's breath away. Never mind that she was well beyond the first blush of youth. "Age cannot wither her, nor custom stale," Shakespeare had once written. Well, actually Lady Hastings wasn't all *that* old. The point was, she seemed the reincarnation of Cleopatra—or Helen—or Calypso—any of those females equipped to lure men to their dooms. A young Denholm would never have stood a chance. With a sinking sensation in her stomach pit, Antonia watched the seductively mocking smile play on the beauty's lips as she studied her ex-lover. "I see this is your hat, Fitzhugh." Her voice was warm and husky. "I can't imagine how you came to lose it." Her knowing smile belied her words.

"No, but I'm sure you'll try, Eugenia," he answered levelly, taking it from her but managing to avoid the intended contact with her hand. "Thank you very much." He clapped the beaver on his head, then tipped it. "Your servant, Eugenia. Captain."

But Lady Hastings reached across and seized his arm before he could flick the reins. "Please, Fitzhugh," she pleaded softly. "Don't run away. You've avoided me at every turn. Refused my letters." The lovely dark eyes brimmed with tears. "It isn't like you to be so cruel. All I ask is a few minutes of your time. And I should not ask that if it were not absolutely vital. If Miss Thorpe would change places with me. You would not mind, would you, Miss Thorpe?"

"Oh, not in the least," Antonia managed to say with forced politeness. But as she started to climb down, a vise-like grip on her arm prevented it. How absurd we must look, she thought inanely, she holding him, he, me.

"Miss Thorpe may not mind, Eugenia, but I do." Denholm's voice was still coolly civil, but he shook the beauty's hand off as though it were some species of vermin that had landed on his sleeve. "As I have endeavored to make clear—but then, you always were a bit obtuse—we've nothing at all to say to each other."

He sprang the horses so abruptly that Antonia feared her neck had snapped. She bit back a protest just in case he proved dangerous. There was no doubt about it, Mr. Denholm was in high dudgeon. She longed to repeat his maxim: A good whip never takes out his anger on his cattle. But she bit that back as well. Antonia was learning prudence fast.

But when he halted his winded team in front of Thirkell House, she considered the tension eased enough to ask, "Don't you think you were rather rough on Lady Hastings?"

His look almost blasted her off the seat. "No, I do not."

"It wouldn't have hurt you to talk to her a minute."

"You know nothing of the matter." He jumped down and reached up an impatient hand to help her alight.

"I know she loves you. All of London knows that."

"And I would be grateful if you and all of London would stay out of my affairs. Good day, Miss Thorpe."

He nodded curtly, climbed into the curricle, and cracked his whip, leaving her standing on the cobblestones, gazing thoughtfully after him as he recklessly took the corner on two wheels.

Arriving back in his own lodgings did little to improve Denholm's mood. The brandy his man presented him might have helped if it had not been accompanied on the silver tray by a letter from his father. Denholm read the epistle twice before consigning it to the fire.

The news of the London theatrical sensation had filtered down to Kent. This latest chapter in Fitzhugh's sordid history had put his mother to bed, so his father had informed him, and might well prove to be more than her much-tried constitution could overcome. As for his lordship, his son would never know the pain and humiliation that gentleman had suffered, for unlike Fitzhugh, he cringed at making a public spectacle of himself.

The point of the letter was not to dwell upon his or his dear wife's pain, however, his father continued, but to consider what might be done to salvage the few shreds of dignity left the Denholm name. So after talking the matter over with Sir Edwin Thorpe (there had been several lines devoted to Sir Edwin's magnanimous attitude; not every gentlemen would wish to see his daughter married to a man lumbered with such scandal), they had decided that the quickest way to stop tongues wagging was for Society to read the notice of the Honorable Fitzhugh Denholm's betrothal in the *Gazette*. That should scotch all speculation about an alliance between Fitzhugh and "that woman." Sir Edwin was writing to let his daughter know his wishes in the matter. Instead of finishing out the London Season, Miss Thorpe was to accept Fitzhugh's proposal and come home. Lord Worth concluded by hoping he might rely upon his son to respect his father's wishes in this one matter and offer for Miss Rosamond Thorpe with all dispatch.

After the letter had flamed, curled into black carbon, and then disintegrated, Denholm sat for a long time staring into the fire and drinking deep. If the desired numbness didn't come to alleviate some of the pain that he was feeling, at least the brandy, or time, brought resignation.

Perhaps marrying Rosamond Thorpe was the best thing that could happen. It would be a marriage of convenience, in the classic mode—"convenient" for both of them to see as little of each other as the business of producing an heir would allow. True, having to give up her curate might go hard with Rosamond for a while. But Denholm was well enough acquainted with that spoiled young lady to know that life with an impoverished cleric would not suit her for very long. Of course, her father wouldn't likely leave her destitute. But unless Denholm missed his guess, some of the curate's luster had already begun to fade as Rosamond herself acquired town bronze.

Yes, he and she might deal well enough together. For the fortunate thing was, she didn't love him. A picture of her cousin's face at the conclusion of their kiss came back to haunt him. And despite the way Antonia had rallied her forces to hide her feelings and stop him making a foolish declaration, he was far too worldly not to realize she'd fallen in love with him. And though at this moment his deepest desire was to tell his father to go to blazes, that he planned to marry the other, ineligible Miss Thorpe, he knew he could not do it. Rosamond might appear to be the weaker of the two cousins, but she was well armed against him. She didn't love him. Ergo, he couldn't hurt her. Whereas Antonia was very vulnerable indeed. And while he might think now at this very moment he would, perhaps, be able to make her happy—he refilled his glass and quickly drained it—it was no good. For he had no faith in his constancy at all.

Chapter Sixteen

Sir Edwin Thorpe had not relied upon the mail coach to convey his wishes to his daughter. He had personally come up to London to avoid any misunderstanding.

There was none. But after he had gone, poor Rosamond was in such a quake over Mr. Denholm's looming proposal that she sent a message at once to Captain Crosland appealing for his help. It was his advice that she absent herself as much as possible from Wimpole Street until they could work out a strategy. Mr. Denholm could hardly propose if he could not find her home.

The two sought out Antonia. "I'm convinced Denholm really loves Lady Hastings" was Captain Crosland's voiced opinion. "We merely have to get them together long enough for her to break down his stiff-necked pride. Eugenia has suggested that we arrange an outing with him to Vauxhall."

"Oh, but I couldn't go there." Rosamond looked shocked. The gardens, a favorite gathering place for the hoi polloi, had gained a rather unsavory reputation.

"Not you, Miss Rosamond. I rely upon your cousin to persuade Mr. Denholm to take her to Vauxhall Gardens."

The captain overrode all of Antonia's objections. "In the first place," she'd protested, "I can't really accept your premise that Mr. Denholm is in love with Lady Hastings.

You observed him in the park. I'd come nearer to believing he hated her."

"Of course that's how it appeared. You should know that there's a fine line between love and hate. Now, if he were indifferent, that would be quite another matter."

"Perhaps you're right," she reluctantly conceded. "But in the second place, I doubt I can persuade him to go."

"Of course you can." Rosamond's eyes were large and trusting. "Mr. Denholm quite likes you, Antonia."

So in the end she had agreed to try and lure Mr. Denholm to Vauxhall Gardens, since they'd come up with no other plan. "It will have to be quite soon," the practical captain pointed out. "Rosamond can only dodge Denholm for a few more days before her father learns of it."

Her cousin's touching gratitude for her cooperation made Antonia squirm. For as much as she was sickened by the thought of Denholm married to Lady Hastings, she liked the thought of his being married to Rosamond even less. Hence her willingness to help.

The following day their silly scheme seemed even more rackety, however, and she decided to postpone sending a message to Mr. Denholm until afternoon. He'd not likely stir from bed all morning anyhow. In the meantime she could be thinking how best to persuade him to accompany her to Vauxhall. And, she decided, a visit to Spring Gardens might clear her brain for that distasteful effort and at the same time lift her sagging spirits. So after receiving permission from Lady Thirkell, Antonia engaged the coachman to drive her to Pimlico.

The drawing exhibition there had the desired effect of wiping everything else but its beauty from her mind as she walked through the various rooms studying the array of paintings jammed together upon the walls—three, four, even five deep, depending upon the size. Antonia craned her neck to observe those next to the ceiling and squatted ungracefully to examine those near the floor. Then when fatigue finally broke through her absorption, she seated herself at a table provided in the center of the room and settled in to concentrate on those works of the late, great Sir Joshua Reynolds that were grouped within her view.

After spending some time trying to commit the artist's techniques to memory, Antonia had a better notion. She laid her sketchbook open on the table, helped herself to the pen and ink so thoughtfully provided, and with frowning concentration began to draw.

"That's not bad." The voice that caused her to spoil a line sounded surprised. "You never told me you were an artist." The Honorable Fitzhugh Denholm sat down beside her and cast an appraising eye over her sketch, then studied it intently. "Not bad," he repeated. "Perhaps if you tried this, however." He took the pen from her nerveless fingers and with a few deft strokes altered her drawing until it reflected the essence of the masterpiece upon the wall.

"Damnation," Antonia said.

Denholm looked slightly shocked. "I do beg pardon. I've spoiled the picture for you. I had no right."

"No, you haven't spoiled it. Quite the contrary, in fact." She was mortified at her unladylike exclamation. "It's just so aggravating. Is there anything you can't do?"

"Oh, the list is endless."

"It doesn't seem to be." Her disgust got the upper hand again. "Here I was, thinking seriously that my greatest asset was an ability to draw and that perhaps I could employ myself by giving lessons; then you happen along and with five strokes of the pen show me how absurd my notion was."

"Oh, come now. You make me feel like a monster. I said your work was good."

"Actually, what you said was that it wasn't bad. Then clearly demonstrated that it was. There's no use hoping anyone will take me seriously as an artist when any foppish"—she stared pointedly at the brand-new coat of bottle-green he wore, set off by a flowery buttonhole—"dilettante who comes along can immediately outdo me."

140

"No need to be insulting. I said I was sorry." His twinkling eyes, however, belied a true repentance. "Besides, I take exception to your name-calling. Oh, I grant you 'foppish.' Weston will be pleased that you noticed his latest creation. It's all the crack. And my valet insisted on the buttonhole. But I'm no dilettante." He had reclaimed her sketchbook and was drawing furiously with one eye on the wall. "Some people would say that I can even out-Reynolds Reynolds." He pushed the drawing toward her, and she laughed out loud, causing heads to turn curiously their way. What he had produced was an absurdly comical caricature of the artist's work "Mrs. Siddons as the Tragic Muse."

"Oh, really, this is libelous!" Antonia whispered. "Poor Sir Joshua is no doubt turning in his—" She broke off suddenly to stare at him. "That was your cartoon at the printshop, wasn't it?"

"Damnation!" It was his turn to voice disgust. He didn't pretend not to know exactly what she meant.

"It never occurred to me—or to anyone else, I daresay—that you'd done that wicked drawing."

"I hope not. And I'd appreciate your keeping it to yourself. I was immediately sorry for it. It was a petty—womanish, if you'll forgive me—sort of revenge."

" 'Womanish'!" she bristled. "Well, perhaps you're right. It was subtle. And funny. And made its point. What would 'manly' be? A duel? That was your earlier recourse, as I recall."

He studied her thoughtfully. "You really do have your dagger drawn today, haven't you? But since you bring it up, actually I've never been enamored of the art of dueling; though, if you'll forgive my adding to your grievances, I am good at it. But my only indulgence in that activity was forced upon me.

"What I should have preferred to do after I saw that play was plant a few levelers. I'm also good at that. But one can't hit a weakling. And certainly not a female. Hence

141

the cartoon. Oh, yes, I got drunk as well. Neither reaction very laudable, I fear.''

''Maybe not. But still a great improvement over pistols at dawn.''

''Don't patronize me. But to get back to our earlier discussion, and none too soon, I don't see why my ability, or lack of it, with a pen should have anything to say to your ambitions to be a drawing teacher. My superiority to you in that area is doubtful. Sir Joshua's . . .''—he nodded toward the wall—''is an established fact. You didn't let him discourage you. Why me? It makes no sense.''

''It certainly does. I can't even compete with amateurs.''

''Forgive—once again—my immodesty. I'm not precisely that. That is, if you define 'professional' as one who's paid and don't judge by quality: you see, I did work as an illustrator in Italy.''

She stared in amazement. ''Did you really?''

''Oh, yes. I've several books to my credit. Or 'discredit,' if you will. Again I rely on your discretion. I'd hate for my father to learn of this other blot on the Denholm escutcheon. He would probably find my venture into commerce a greater disgrace than my womanizing. At least, there's precedent among the ton for the latter pursuit.''

''Your father is sap-skulled, if you'd pardon my saying so. I think what you did is famous. Oh, I know—you informed me when we first met that I'm little better than a cit. So, I suppose my attitude only proves your point. But I really don't see how anyone, gentleman or not, could bear to be forever idle. I'm glad you found something interesting to occupy you while you were abroad. For I don't suppose,'' she added thoughtfully, ''that even the grandest passion would make one wish to make love exclusively and have no other interests.''

''One does reach a saturation point,'' he observed with a near-straight face.

''I shouldn't have said that either.'' She sighed. ''But I do find it difficult to stand on points with you. From the

142

moment we met, our association has been so—bizarre—that it seems impossible to put things back on a proper footing."

"Antonia, I would not have you changed for all of China's tea."

"You're roasting me, of course. I realize I should change. But it hardly seems worth the effort since I doubt we shall be seeing each other very much longer." This observation struck Antonia as such a lowering prospect, that she rushed on to say, "Do tell me, please, how does one become an illustrator? Do you think I'm good enough to do it? Does it pay well? I must say it sounds a great deal more pleasant than instructing children. Don't you agree?"

Denholm seemed almost as anxious as she to move the conversation from the muddied waters of their relationship. He willingly launched into a discourse upon the illustrator's craft, which he concluded with a promise to explore the London possibilities for her. And as Antonia was expressing her gratitude for his offer, she suddenly recalled the mission she'd been entrusted with. "Oh, dear. This is terrible," she blurted out. "I've another favor to ask of you. Will you escort me to Vauxhall Gardens tomorrow night?"

"No. Nor at any other time."

"No? Oh, dear. I did so very much wish to go there." Antonia fairly choked on the whisker. "And Lady Thirkell will only give her permission if you take me."

"Then, my aunt has taken complete leave of her senses. Vauxhall Gardens is no place for you. And particularly not with me."

"Oh, but you would be the perfect escort. You've just admitted that you're a dab hand in a mill. You'd be well able to protect me against any rough element I might meet there."

"Yes, but who'd protect you from me?"

"Don't be absurd. I'll need no such protection. Not un-

143

less we drive in your curricle and race someone on the way. That's the only time we behave improperly.''

Her attempt at humor failed. There was no responsive smile. "I'll not take you to Vauxhall." Denholm rose to his feet. "It's no place for a lady. Trust my judgment on that score at least. My aunt is out of touch, or she wouldn't dream of encouraging you to go there. Not with anyone."

Antonia looked so distressed that he reached out and lightly touched her cheek. "I wouldn't disappoint you without good reason, Tonia." He smiled crookedly. "You really must learn not to play with fire. Good day."

He turned abruptly and strode from the gallery, leaving Antonia confused as to whether it was Vauxhall or himself he was warning her away from.

Chapter Seventeen

Rosamond threatened hysterics when she learned of Antonia's failure and was warned that if she didn't hush that instant Mrs. Blakeney was sure to reappear to see what was wrong. Captain Crosland, though, received the news that Mr. Denholm had flatly refused to escort Miss Thorpe to Vauxhall Gardens with surprising equanimity. He and Rosamond had come calling at Grosvenor Square that afternoon to find out if Antonia had succeeded in contacting Mr. Denholm (and, not incidentally, to insure that if the Honorable Fitzhugh Denholm came calling at Wimpole Street, he'd find Rosamond out). They were in the withdrawing room huddled over the tea tray, deep in conspiracy.

"Don't be distressed," the captain spoke soothingly to Rosamond. "No campaigner goes into battle without a contingency plan. If Denholm had agreed to accompany Miss Antonia, it would have made matters simpler, that's all. But it will amount to the same thing in the end. And that's what counts. Miss Antonia, I will personally escort you to the gardens. Lady Hastings can make her own arrangements."

"But what's the point of going without Denholm?" Antonia protested.

"He'll be there. Leave that to me."

"But I needn't be. And I certainly do not wish to."

"Oh, but you, Miss Antonia, are absolutely vital to my scheme. Now here's what we shall do."

Antonia thought little of the captain's plan, which involved sending Denholm a note, supposedly from Lady Thirkell, saying that Miss Thorpe had gone without her permission to Vauxhall and asking him to set out in hot pursuit.

"What if Denholm is not at home?" she objected.

"Why, then, the footman will track him down."

"But what if Mr. Denholm checks first with Lady Thirkell?"

"The note will make it clear that he should waste no time in rescuing a foolish young lady from the perils of Vauxhall."

After more debate along similar lines, Antonia returned to her main objection. The purpose of the exercise was to throw Lady Hastings and Mr. Denholm together. Why was it necessary for her to actually go to Vauxhall?

By this time the captain's patience had worn thin. "There's no need at all if you're willing to have Mr. Denholm know you've plotted the whole thing."

"He'll know anyhow."

"Why should he? You've convinced him you wish to visit Vauxhall. He wouldn't take you. I'm more accommodating. The fact that Lady Hastings will just happen to visit the gardens that night is sheer coincidence."

"Why doesn't Rosamond come, too?"

Her cousin looked shocked. "Papa would kill me."

"We don't want Rosamond there reminding Denholm of where his duty lies, now, do we? Really, Miss Antonia, I certainly don't claim my plan is foolproof. But your cousin does not have much time. The only way I can see to prevent her disastrous marriage is to bring about this reconciliation. Now, if you have a better idea of how to achieve that, we'll try it."

But in the end, all their scheming proved academic. For Denholm had a sudden change of heart. He kept remembering how upset Antonia had seemed when he'd refused to take her to Vauxhall. But most of all he kept remembering how she'd said they'd not be seeing each other much longer. He was surprised at just how blue-deviled that prospect made him feel. And so, he'd gone calling on his great-aunt the following day.

Lady Thirkell looked over her spectacles in surprise and put down her needlework. "Well, Fitzhugh, it's been a long time since I've entertained a handsome gentleman in my bedchamber. To what do I owe this honor?"

"I'd like a private word, ma'am." He refused the offer of tea and, ignoring the chair she indicated, went wandering about the room, picking up bits of bric-a-brac, examining the reading material by her bedside, pulling back the damask curtains to peer out the window, and, finally, inquiring absently about her health.

"At eighty-two my health is precarious, Fitzhugh" was the testy answer. "There's a good chance I may not survive long enough for you to disclose the purpose of your visit. Do sit down. You're making me positively giddy."

He grinned and obediently plopped down in a carved and gilt armchair, a twin to the one she sat in. "I was trying to find a subtle way to worm some information without you knowing what I was up to. I give up."

"And a good thing, too. I admit to old, but deny senility. Come to the point, lad."

"I want to ask about your will."

"So, that's the way the wind blows." She gave him a hard look above her spectacles. "Strapped then, are you? Wondering if I've made you me heir?"

"No, of course not, to both questions. Oh, the devil! I am making a mull of this. But you don't actually think I'm after your fortune, do you? Good God, such a thing never occurred to me. I may not be the nabob you are, Aunt, but I'm quite plump in the pocket, thank you."

"Is that so? Heard a rumor that old Paxton bypassed Worth and left you his fortune. True, then?"

147

"As a matter of fact, yes."

She chuckled wickedly. "Lord, I wish I could have seen Worth's face when he found out. Paxton never could abide him, now I recall it. Thought your father too platter-faced by half. And he was right. Even as a boy Worth was a hopeless prig. And your Uncle Paxton always did have a soft spot for rogues."

"Thank you."

"Oh, you're welcome. But if you've no need for a fortune, clear up this mystery. Why on earth are you dangling after that insufferable Thorpe chit?"

"Which one?"

"Don't be impudent. You know perfectly well I would never describe Antonia so. I mean Rosamond, of course. Do you intend to marry her?"

"Yes."

"For God's sake, why? You'll never suit."

"We should rub along as well as most couples, I collect. But I did not come here to talk of my affairs."

"It's Worth, I suppose. You two have been at daggers drawn ever since you came out of leading strings. Seems a bit late to try to please him now. But never mind. Before you wish me to the devil I'll admit it's none of my affair. But now then, sir, suppose you tell me just why you're poking your nose into what is my affair. My will, I mean."

"I'm wondering if you've left Mrs. Blakeney provided for."

"No, of course not" was the acid rejoinder. "I've consigned her to the workhouse. Good God, boy, what do you take me for? Of course she's provided for. And though I'd like to believe you've developed a touching concern for indigent old ladies, well, I wasn't born yesterday, you know. If it's Antonia you're concerned with, why not say so?"

"It amounts to the same thing, doesn't it?" Denholm, feeling rather guilty as he did so, went on to confide some of Antonia's concerns about the future.

"So her father's remarrying. Hmmm. Antonia did well to hide that from her grandmother. It will break Claire's heart. Though why it should is more than I can say. It's remarkable that Thorpe stayed single this long. Handsome fellow as I recall. But a lightweight. Antonia, thank God, takes after her grandfather. Now, there was a man!"

"He must have been, to maintain two households. I'm sorry. That was in poor taste. From me, especially."

"You'd best apologize. For I'll not hear one word against John. And as for Antonia's future, Claire will be more than able to look out for the girl. Not that it will be necessary. All men aren't fools. Antonia will make a match. Mark me words."

"Oh, undoubtedly you're right." The young man did not appear particularly cheered by this reassurance. "But why don't you do this much, Aunt Kate. Tell Antonia what you've done. Let her know she doesn't have to be forced into marriage just to support herself."

"I'll do no such thing. I don't want the gel feeling obliged to me. Besides, having money doesn't nullify bad marriages. As you're determined to demonstrate."

"Touché. Go ahead and ring for tea if you wish, Aunt Kate. For there's one more thing I want to ask you."

If Lady Thirkell found the concluding part of her tête-à-tête with her great-nephew even more puzzling than the first, she refrained from saying so. Instead she agreed to Denholm's plan with an alacrity that surprised them both.

It was left up to Antonia to express amazement after his departure when she was summoned to the dowager's bedchamber. "Mr. Denholm has invited you, Grandmother, and me to Vauxhall Gardens? Surely not!"

"Not only that, at your grandmother's suggestion, he has expanded the party to include Rosamond and Captain Crosland. I don't wonder you look amazed, m'dear. I know that Vauxhall is no longer considered quite the thing. But there's still some wholesome amusement to be had there.

149

And for a party such as ours, well the outing must be considered unexceptionable.''

"Oh, I am sure of that, ma'am." Antonia struggled not to laugh.

Captain Crosland, however, did not share her sense of the ridiculous, as he made clear on the evening of their expedition while he, Antonia, and Rosamond stood waiting for the others to join them in the hall. "Oh, come now," Antonia protested when the captain had refused to abandon his plan to bring Lady Hastings and Mr. Denholm together. "You surely don't think you can insinuate Lady Hastings into our group. With Lady Thirkell and Grandmama? That's too absurd.''

"Of course not. We will not include Eugenia Hastings. We shall simply rid ourselves of Denholm, which sounds simpler, I must say, than luring him there would have been. You should be able to detach him from our party with little difficulty.''

"Me!" she squeaked as his choice of pronoun sunk in.

"Shhh!" He frowned and shook his head. Lady Thirkell and Mrs. Blakeney, escorted by their host for the evening's outing, were coming down the stairs, Mrs. Blakeney touching the banister lightly and Lady Thirkell gaining moral support, at least, from both her nephew and her cane.

If Antonia had not already anticipated an awkward evening, the business of disposing themselves in her ladyship's old-fashioned crested coach would have pointed in that direction. Lady Thirkell had a fear of drafts. Mrs. Blakeney could not ride backward without getting ill. Rosamond seemed determined not to sit by Denholm. In the end, Lady Thirkell, tightly enveloped in a fur-lined cloak, even though the evening was actually warm for May, sat flanked by her companion and her nephew, facing forward, her knees all but touching Crosland's. Antonia herself spent the entire time of the seemingly endless journey trying to look anywhere but straight into Denholm's eyes.

But in spite of all, once Denholm had paid the two shillings apiece admission price and ushered them inside, Antonia found herself enjoying Vauxhall. As long as she could forget their covert reason for being there, it was easy to become entranced by the brilliantly illuminated walks where myriads of tiny colored lamps decorated trees and arches, where pavilions glittered, water cascaded, and romantic grottoes abounded. They strolled leisurely along, being entertained by jugglers, rope dancers, tumblers, and sword swallowers, pausing now and again to refresh themselves at the various stands or to purchase souvenirs at exorbitantly high prices. Rosamond declared Vauxhall the most famous place she had yet seen in London and Lady Thirkell unbent so far as to congratulate her nephew for arranging such a treat.

Captain Crosland seemed the only one of the conspirators whose mind remained fixed on their main objective. The fatigued party had gathered for supper in one of the long rows of boxes provided for that purpose and were partaking of the chicken, beef, and proverbially thin slices of ham that Vauxhall was noted for, the gentlemen washing the food down with the equally famous Vauxhall Nectar, a mixture of rum and syrup with an addition of flowers of Benjamin. When a nearby band struck up a raucous tune, the captain, who had abandoned Rosamond for the first time that evening to sit beside Antonia, whispered in her ear, "You can make your move during the fireworks display."

Really, Antonia thought, he was the most impossible man! From his cloak-and-dagger approach they might be planning to stab Caesar.

"What move?" she whispered back, annoyed with herself as well when she waited for a covering drumroll to do so.

"When we go to watch the fireworks," he instructed from behind a concealing apple tart, "you must lure Denholm away to the Dark Walk."

"What!" Antonia forgot to whisper and as a result had

her soft shoe nudged none too gently by a Hessian boot. She noticed Denholm watching them curiously from down the table and just managed to tone down her "Ow!"

"I can't do that," she hissed as Denholm turned his attention back to Rosamond, who was keeping up a constant stream of chatter in his ear, fearing to pause lest he make an offer of marriage then and there. "I could never make such a shocking proposal. What would he think?"

"If he's the man I take him for," the other said, leering "he'll jump at the notion. But don't look so horrified. You won't actually have to go on the Dark Walk with him. Lady Hastings will be waiting there. You can slip back before you're even missed."

Antonia had not actually made up her mind to go through with Crosland's rackety scheme, but then fate seemed to conspire against her better judgment. At ten o'clock, when all the pleasure-seekers gathered to watch the fireworks display, the crush was so great that it became impossible for their party to stay together. Antonia was elbowed aside by a law clerk with a wife and brood of children intent upon a better vantage point to view the pyrotechnics. Mr. Denholm was the only member of their group left in the vicinity.

Together they watched the sky come alive in myriad fiery patterns, bursting, twirling, cascading, as if the firmament had marshaled all its stars and planets to appear at once, then caused them to go berserk for their amusement. Antonia could have been content to stand spellbound, but duty nagged her. And so she screwed her courage to the sticking place and tugged at Denholm's sleeve to drag his attention earthward. "Could we go to the Dark Walk now?" Her smile was meant to be provocative.

"I beg your pardon?" A rapid series of explosions had made Denholm doubt his ears.

"I'm longing to see the Dark Walk. Could you take me? Now?"

152

He gestured toward the heavens, where the spectacle defied belief. "Are you bored, Miss Thorpe?"

"No, of course not. It's just that the Dark Walk is the most famous part of Vauxhall Gardens, and if we don't slip away now while my grandmother's attention is on the fireworks, I'll not get to see it. I doubt that she'd approve."

"So do I," he answered dryly. "You do know why people go there?"

"Of course." She tried to sound coquettish. It was hard to tell from his expression whether the performance was convincing. He was studying her intently.

"Come on, then." He made up his mind abruptly and took her hand. They weaved their way in silence through the throng.

As they finally broke clear Antonia walked swiftly. "You are eager," he commented.

"Well, I don't dare be gone long." He still held her hand, but she was almost dragging him.

"Then, I suggest we change directions. The Dark Walk's this way." He gave a jerk that prevented her from taking a wrong path in the mazelike garden.

The lovers' rendezvous was well named, Antonia discovered as they left all the sparkle and glitter behind them. The effect should have been romantic, mysterious; somehow it missed the mark.

"Scared?" Denholm inquired.

"No, of course not," she answered stoutly, but clung more tightly to his hand nonetheless.

They were approaching the entrance to the walk where the thick foliage that lined the path obscured what little light had managed to seep into the surrounding area. The squeals and giggles coming from behind the hedges made it all too clear that they were not the only ones to take advantage of the general preoccupation with the fireworks. It was all in the spirit of fun, of course, Antonia told herself. No need to feel it was somehow demeaning, perhaps disgraceful even.

"Want to go back? You can always say you've seen the Dark Walk?"

"Oh, no. 'In for a penny, in for a pound.' We have to go inside." She led the way into the entrance.

The giggles were funneled toward them now. Punctuated with an occasional playful slap. And there were other sounds she did not care to identify. She also closed her ears to the suggestive remarks that came from some young men lounging back against the hedges, waiting for unescorted female prey.

"Don't you think we've gone far enough, Antonia? I hardly think this is your sort of thing."

"Just a little farther." She led him on with grim determination. Where was Lady Hastings anyhow? She should have been near the entrance. Antonia was feeling more like Theseus in search of the Minotaur. And then, just as she'd decided that in all good conscience they could now turn back, they rounded a bend where the hedges formed a grotto with a convenient bench for lovers, and there in the gloom sat a female figure who rose slowly to her feet as they approached.

"Ah, there you are at last." Lady Hastings's voice was husky, sultry. "I'd almost despaired of seeing you, Fitzhugh."

Antonia felt Denholm stiffen. His grip on her hand now made her wince. "So, that's what this has been about all along, Miss Thorpe," he said softly between clenched teeth. She was thankful the darkness made his expression difficult to read.

"Miss Thorpe has been a dear friend, Fitzhugh." As the beauty moved toward them, Antonia stepped away, or tried to. The grip on her hand increased. "She knew I'd perish if I didn't get to talk to you—to make things right again." Lady Hastings pressed against him. Her hands rested on his shoulders. Her eyes gazed imploringly into his. "Oh,

154

Fitz, my darling, you can't stay angry always. You know you're the only man I've ever loved.'' She suddenly grew aware of his appendage and spoke sharply. "You can go now, Miss Thorpe. I'm ever so grateful to you.''

"By all means, Miss Thorpe.'' Denholm dropped Antonia's hand like loosing a hot coal. "Your decoy duty is over. May I congratulate you on a job well done?''

Antonia ran. Tears stung her eyes and made seeing impossible. She blundered into the hedge as the path curved. Why she should feel like a Judas defied all understanding. Cupid was the role she'd meant to play. Or maybe that was what made her so miserable. She'd succeeded all too well, and it was herself that she'd betrayed.

"Got you!'' Rough arms seized Antonia. A male body pressed hard against her own. A dim face leered. She smelled the brandy-breath as the parted mouth bent toward her. She screamed. Then screamed again and struggled but was quickly overpowered. Her arms were pinned. The slack, wet mouth met hers with a repulsiveness that sickened, made her long to faint even while she knew that she could not. She kicked and stamped, but the soft shoes she wore made such tactics ineffectual—mere annoyances that only served to increase her assailant's passion. Then, just when it seemed she might succeed in fainting after all, her attacker was jerked roughly around and a well-aimed blow sent him buckling to his knees.

"Come on.'' Denholm tugged her by the hand. "If you've had quite enough of the Dark Walk, Miss Thorpe, I'll return you to your party.''

He rushed her along the path so fast she felt her feet might fly out from under her. She kept rubbing at her mouth with the sleeve of her walking dress, thinking never to rid herself of the feel of those disgusting lips. When they emerged into the open, Denholm pulled out a handkerchief and gave it to her, watching in silence while she rubbed her lips till they were almost raw. "Come on," he said abruptly, not taking her hand again.

155

"You mustn't leave Lady Hastings alone in there," she gasped. "It isn't safe."

"Your concern is touching. Eugenia will manage. She always does. She can fend off all comers till I get back."

"Oh, you are going back, then?" They were hurrying toward the crowd. The fireworks were building to a grand finale.

"Of course. That was the general idea, wasn't it? The motivation behind your burning desire to visit Vauxhall—and all your eagerness to explore, with me, the Dark Walk? Oh, you are quite a matchmaker, Miss Thorpe. Again, my congratulations.

"I see Crosland over there." He pointed toward the tall captain's curly beaver, which stood out above the crowd. "You can make it the rest of the way on your own, I'm sure. Convey my apologies to my guests for leaving them so abruptly. I'm sure you'll think of some explanation for my boorishness. Deception seems to be your forte, Miss Thorpe."

Chapter Eighteen

"Oh, what are we to do, Antonia?" Rosamond wailed. The curate's appeal was no less desperate for being mute; his face was just as stricken. The three of them had met, as arranged, in the lending library. And the star-crossed lovers were gazing at Antonia as if she were their last frail hope. She longed to shake them.

"The only thing to do is what you should have done in the first place. I don't know how we ever allowed ourselves to meddle so in Mr. Denholm's affairs." All they'd accomplished, it seemed, was to make him despise her.

"But Captain Crosland was so sure," Rosamond protested. "And Lady Hastings was so sure that Mr. Denholm truly loved her. It only seemed a matter of simply throwing them together. No one could have known he'd bite his nose off to spite his face."

"Pride is indeed a deadly sin." The curate was perhaps thinking of next Sunday's homily.

"Oh, Antonia"—Rosamond took up the thread again— "Captain Crosland says Denholm actually told Lady Hastings he wants her out of his life once and for all. He p-plans to marry me. That's what he said. And I can't go on avoiding him forever. What shall I do?"

"Run off and get married right away."

"You mean elope?" Rosamond seemed horrified.

"Of course. Really, if you had simply done so ages ago, none of this mess need have happened."

"We wouldn't have made our come-outs either," Rosamond retorted. "Besides, an elopement's quite out of the question."

"Why should it be?" The cousins were coming close to daggers drawn. Antonia had lost all patience with anyone who, if too great a fool to wish to marry Fitzhugh Denholm, was also too fainthearted to run off with the suitor of her choice. "Oh, your father will cut up rough for a while, but he'll come around. You're his only child. He's hardly likely to cut you off with just a shilling."

"Do you know, Rosamond," the curate said thoughtfully, "I think your cousin is right. Believe me, your aversion to elopement does you credit. And you can surmise how repugnant such a course seems to a man of the cloth like myself. But nothing," he said, his voice choked with emotion, "is as repugnant to me as the thought of you married to another."

It should have been a touching moment. Certainly Rosamond seemed deeply moved. Perhaps it was unworthy of Antonia to feel that Rosamond's inheritance was the motive for the curate's decision to throw caution to the wind.

"Well, Rosamond, what have you decided?" She sounded far too brusque and businesslike. But those two might go on gazing soulfully at each other the remainder of the day. "Is it Gretna Green or not?"

"Oh, I don't know." Poor Rosamond struggled with her conscience. "It just does not seem the thing to do."

"Well then, I promised to go shopping with Grandmother at Grafton House. I must be going."

Rosamond caught her hand as she stood up. "Oh, Tonia, don't be angry. Stay just a moment longer. I've decided now. I will do it. Cecil, we shall go to Gretna Green!"

But once that monumental decision had finally been reached, it seemed that the romantic pair hadn't the slightest notion of how to set about eloping. They turned their

158

imploring eyes once more upon Antonia. "Oh, really!" she snapped. "This is the outside of enough. I must be going. You two work it out." Simultaneously their faces fell; then Rosamond suddenly brightened and clapped her hands. "Oh, I know! I shall consult with Captain Crosland. He is an expert when it comes to planning any sort of action. He's bound to tell us exactly how we must proceed."

Antonia's relief at shifting the burden of responsibility to the captain's broad shoulders proved short-lived. He sent round a note early the next morning saying he'd be in the library at ten and it was absolutely imperative that she meet him there. And though the assignation filled her with foreboding, it seemed craven not to go.

I do hope he won't ask me to break the news to Uncle Edwin, she thought as she hurried toward the library, after sending her maid off on an errand to Wedgwood and Byerley's in York Street. Surely, though, Rosamond will leave a note.

It was far worse than she'd imagined. "Go along on the elopement! You're funning, of course." She looked across the library table at the captain's face for a sign of the jokester's twinkle.

The captain, though, was serious. Rosamond absolutely refused to make the journey to Scotland without a chaperone, he told her.

"But Mr. Hollingsworth intends to make an honest woman of her! How ridiculous!"

The captain shrugged and allowed himself a tiny smile. "I fully agree. But then, you're aware of Miss Rosamond's excessive sensibility. She is, after all, Sir Edwin's daughter."

"And has Sir Edwin's daughter thought of how I'm to get back to London with *my* character intact? Oh, never mind." The question was academic. No need to worry about the local gossipmongers, for she'd made up her mind to return to Belgium as soon as possible anyhow. Papa and his new bride might not welcome her with open arms, but they'd have to take her in. And the arrangement would be a temporary thing. It would be far easier, she'd decided, to find a position as a drawing mistress among the English expatriates than here in London. The standards could not be nearly as high.

She listened intently, if reluctantly, as the captain went on to explain in a low voice the plan that he and Rosamond had agreed on. Antonia must say that she intended to spend the following night with Rosamond. Rosamond would tell her Aunt Lydia that Antonia had invited her to stay the night in Grosvenor Square. That way neither would be missed for several hours. In the meantime they would meet tomorrow afternoon at one o'clock in Oxford Street, where the Reverend Hollingsworth would pick them up in a hackney coach.

"One o'clock!" Crosland glanced at the people milling about the library and frowned a warning at Antonia, who lowered her voice. "Shouldn't we be leaving early in the morning? We can't travel at night. There'll be no moon."

The captain had a bit of difficulty keeping his face straight. "I pointed that out, thinking Miss Rosamond would wish to avoid an extra night in an inn. But she wouldn't be budged. She's ordered some new gowns and refuses to leave London till they're delivered sometime tomorrow morning."

"Saints preserve us!" Antonia echoed a favorite expression of her ladyship's Irish maid. Then she caught the captain's eye, and they both dissolved in laughter. She was to recall the reaction later on and wonder how she could have found anything at all amusing in the situation. Disgust would have been the emotion of choice, if only she had known.

After a near sleepless night when she'd tossed and turned, then definitely decided she would not go with Rosamond to Scotland, Antonia wound up arriving early for their rendezvous. She felt most conspicuous backed up

160

against a shop window with a portmanteau in her hand. She prayed that she'd see no acquaintance who might expect an explanation.

When a nearby clock struck the hour of one, and neither Rosamond nor the chaise had appeared, Antonia did not know whether to be relieved or angry. Then, when she saw her cousin hurrying toward her, lumbered with no more than a reticule, relief predominated. Rosamond had obviously changed her mind.

"Of course we're going." Rosamond looked bewildered by her cousin's greeting. "I'm here, am I not?" Then, when Antonia pointed out that the bride had not brought along a traveling bag, Rosamond seemed convinced the other had taken leave of her senses. "I could not possibly marry and take a honeymoon with just the clothes I could cram into a portmanteau. That really would be shocking. I packed all my boxes myself and put them in the carriage house," she said with a touch of pride. "Captain Crosland slipped them out last night and will see to it they are put aboard the coach."

Captain Crosland's responsibilities did not end there, however. When the hackney coach came rattling down the street a few moments later, Antonia glanced briefly at the coachman, then jerked her head back to stare. "Crosland's driving!" she gasped.

"Yes. It's so kind of him. Cecil does not know how, you see."

The coach had pulled to a stop in front of them. The curate peeped out a furtive head, glanced around, saw that the coast was clear, then jumped out and practically pushed his fiancée inside. "Oh, do hurry, Miss Thorpe," he snapped at Antonia.

But she had balked. "It is one thing," she snapped back, "to accompany you and Rosamond. It is quite another to make a foursome with Captain Crosland all the way to Scotland. To say nothing of the fact that the two of us must come back alone. I'll not do it."

The result of this declaration was to send Rosamond into hysterics. "Now see what you've done!" the harassed bridegroom hissed. Passing shoppers were turning to stare their way curiously. The coachman climbed down to join them.

"I know my being here's a shock, Miss Thorpe," he said soothingly. "But Miss Rosamond did not want a hired coachman along who'd make her uncomfortable and gossip later. And Hollingsworth, you see, doesn't drive." The captain sounded scornful.

"Well, I can and will." Antonia's pronouncement only served to increase her cousin's hysteria. As far as an inconspicuous departure went, the elopement was proving to be a dismal failure.

"I can understand and sympathize with your attitude, Miss Antonia." Despite all the pressures, the captain took time to be diplomatic. "But I don't think we can discuss the matter here. I know what we'll do!" He snapped his fingers as inspiration struck. "We'll hire a maid—a farmer's wife—a respectable female of some description—at the very first posting house, to accompany us and serve as chaperone."

"B-but—"

The captain forestalled Rosamond's sobbed objection by another masterstroke. "And no fear of any tale-bearing there. We'll give false names. Now, do get in, Miss Thorpe. We're beginning to collect a crowd."

Antonia was to look back on their awkward departure as the best part of the journey north. For, once having begun to weep, Rosamond made no attempt to stem the tide. The clergyman divided his time between patting her hand ineffectively and glaring at Antonia as the cause of her upset.

Then, once they'd left the metropolis behind, the sobs gradually subsided to be replaced with reproaches of another kind. Could Mr. Hollingsworth not have provided them with a better coach? Rosamond weighed the hackney against her father's well-sprung carriage and found it sadly wanting. Really, she had never been so jolted in all her life! The ordeal was giving her the headache. She'd daresay that her cousin had never experienced such an ill-sprung coach, not even on the Continent. "Have you, Antonia?" And not only was the hackney miserably sprung, it was dirty. Heaven only knew what types of people had ridden in it last. If they did not succumb to all sorts of horrid diseases, it would amaze her. And worst of all, the carriage smelled. Really, she felt quite ill. Rosamond clapped her perfumed handkerchief to her nose.

Antonia, who had been gazing sightlessly out the window, absorbed in her own thoughts, awoke to the situation and turned her cousin's way. Goodness, Rosamond was decidedly green. She leaned far out the window and shouted for the captain to stop the coach.

And from then on it was stop-and-go, stop-and-go, with stop predominating. It seemed that the only way Rosamond could possibly tolerate the journey was to leave the coach at frequent intervals, gulp great breaths of air, and sit by the side of the highway till her head stopped swimming and her stomach settled once again. Really, Antonia thought, at this rate we'll not reach Scotland before Christmas. She did not, however, express the thought aloud. Mr. Hollingsworth was less prudent. "Could you not put your mind on other things, Rosamond dear?" There was some justification for the curate's peevishness. They had broken their trip for the third time within the hour. "I find that reciting elevated passages to myself will often blot out discomfort."

This well-meant suggestion brought on a new storm of tears, followed by the announcement that he was too insensitive for words if he did not realize she was doing everything within her power to continue this odious journey. If only he had provided them with a respectable equipage, instead of being so cheeseparing as to expose his betrothed to such excruciating torture.

Despite the impropriety of their situation, Antonia was

thankful now for the captain's presence. His patience was inexhaustible. He seemed to know exactly the right thing to say to calm even the worst of Rosamond's high fidgets. And after several stops to rest along the wayside, he suggested that walking in a nearby field might be more beneficial than simply sitting, and supported the wilting Rosamond with a steadying arm while they paced to and fro, talking earnestly, in the spring-green meadow. Antonia, in the meantime, stood by the horses. The curate stared balefully after them with folded arms.

Then, when the twosome returned from this exercise with Rosamond looking rather more the thing, neither the curate nor Antonia could quarrel with the captain's logic when he suggested they put up at the next posting house they came to, rather than continue on till dark as they had planned. "All of this has put too much strain upon Miss Thorpe's delicate nervous system," he said soothingly. "And it's little wonder. She will be much better for some quiet rest. Then, I daresay, we'll find we can make capital time tomorrow. We'll more than make up for the delay, I promise you. And it's not as if anyone will be chasing after us. We've covered our tracks quite well, I'd say."

Recognizing her cousin's growing dependence upon Captain Crosland, Antonia seized the opportunity to suggest she drive. The curate was aghast at the idea and said so. Rosamond, however, would welcome the captain's comforting presence inside.

"No need to be alarmed, Hollingsworth," he said. "Why, the horses could drive themselves on this stretch of road. I'll take over before we reach the inn." The curate reddened at the patronizing tone.

With this new arrangement in effect, they were actually able to cover the final stretch of the day's journey without stopping. Antonia began, almost, to enjoy herself. Whether due to being freed from Rosamond's complaints, or to the uninterrupted view of the countryside she was afforded from the coachman's perch, or to the fact that it was fun to hold the reins of even these poor specimen of cattle hitched to this much disparaged coach, or to a combination of all these things, this interlude was definitely the high point of her day. She spied the sign of the Old Bull and Horn Inn in the distance but scorned the notion of changing places with Captain Crosland. Her passengers were too self-absorbed to notice that they were about to reach their destination. Before they awakened to that fact, Antonia had tooled the hackney into the crowded inn yard with as much style and dash as such a ramshackle equipage could manage. Curious heads turned, and jaws came crashing down at the sight of a young lady wearing a modish bonnet and stylish pelisse perched on the driver's seat.

But no one in the assembly was half so surprised as Lord Thayer Edgemon. His lordship, in the act of springing his matched grays, froze with his whip in the air to stare at what he at first believed was a hallucination as Captain Crosland came leaping out of the coach to hand Antonia down.

Later on that same evening he expressed some of this astonishment to Mr. Denholm when he happened upon his friend at Brooks's. He had come strolling into the club just as a game of deep basset was breaking up. He and Denholm were now sharing a bowl of punch.

"Damnedest thing," Lord Thayer remarked. "Couldn't believe me eyes at first. Thought I was seeing things. Imagining, you know. But I rubbed me peepers hard and sure enough I was still seeing what I saw."

"Thayer, what are you raving on about?" Denholm was looking rather the worse from too little sleep of late along with having shot the cat a bit too often.

"Trying to tell you of this odd thing I saw, old man." Lord Thayer was noted for his patience. "Was coming back from Derby today. Told you I'd been up to rusticate with Whitcomb, didn't I? Well, then. I'd stopped in at the Old Bull and Horn. Know it, don't you? You can get a damn fine arrack punch there. Well, anyhow, as I was just about to spring me horses, here comes this hackney coach turning into the yard with Miss Antonia Thorpe driving the thing.''

Denholm, who had taken a deep draft of punch, choked suddenly.

"Watch it, Fitz. Damned near sprayed me. New coat, too. Knew you'd be surprised."

"Miss Thorpe driving a hackney!" Denholm expostulated when he'd sufficiently recovered. "The Old Bull and Horn *must* make a damned fine arrack punch."

"Knew you'd not believe it. Didn't myself at first. But told you. I made sure. It was her and no mistake. But you ain't heard the queerest start of all. Guess who got out of the carriage she was driving—bold as brass."

"I've no idea," Denholm said faintly.

"That Captain Crosland, that's who. Friend of yours, perhaps, but frankly I never could quite stomach the fellow. There's something—can't say what exactly—that ain't quite the thing about him."

"Did you speak to them? Find out what they were doing there?"

"Of course not. What do you take me for?" Lord Thayer looked offended. "The very last thing they'd want would be to see, and be seen by, some cove they knew."

Further discussion of this topic was made impossible by three friends who joined them at their table. The conversation soon turned to a mill between Ferocious Frederick and Barton the Bruiser, which was to take place the following week. And though the discussion grew quite heated, Mr. Denholm was not a participant. Indeed, he simply stared off into space for several minutes, then rose, excused himself, and left the room.

Chapter Nineteen

Antonia was roused by a banging on the door. It was broad daylight. She poked her head out from under the pillow where it was buried to see if Rosamond would answer. She, after all, was on the side of the bed nearest the door.

Her cousin was gone. Antonia sighed and reached for her dressing gown as the knocking continued. "Just a minute," she called, and it stopped. Rosamond had locked herself out, no doubt. She had been restless all night long, up and down, up and down, till finally in desperation Antonia had clapped her pillow over her ears and slept. It's going to be another one of those days, she thought as she clutched her robe around her and stumbled toward the door. Since she hadn't gotten the rest Captain Crosland had prescribed, Rosamond was bound to be as difficult as before.

As Antonia opened the door, the curate, fully dressed, pushed past her. "They've gone!" he croaked, waving a sheet of paper in her face.

"Who's gone?" Antonia closed the door, which, even in his agitation, he had left wide open for propriety's sake.

"Rosamond and the captain, you numskull! Who else is with us?"

Antonia looked at Mr. Hollingsworth with some alarm. He was beside himself. "Have you looked in the dining parlor?'' she asked soothingly. ''They're probably just having an early breakfast.''

''They've eloped!'' the curate screeched. ''Of all the underhanded—treacherous—despicable—Here, read this.'' He thrust a paper at her. Antonia frowned down at the hasty scrawl.

My dear Cecil,

Captain Crosland and I have just discovered—quite in the nick of time—that we have loved each other always and have gone on to Gretna Green to be married there. Try and forgive me, Cecil. In time you will come to thank me. As dear Horatio has pointed out, we should not have suited.

Yrs. most truly,
Rosamond

''Good God!'' Antonia sank weakly down upon the bed and reread the letter.

''That cad! That blackguard! He intended this all the time.'' The curate paced up and down the room. Antonia had never actually seen anyone tear his hair before. ''He meant to steal her from me from the very first. The man's nothing but a gazetted fortune hunter.''

''I expect you're right,'' Antonia said thoughtfully.

''And I hold you entirely to blame.''

''Me!''

''He's your friend. You're the one who insinuated him into her life. Nothing has been right since you came to England. Rosamond was always so sweet—so sheltered—so pure. Then you descend upon her with your scandalous background—''

''Scandalous background!'' She was on her feet. ''How dare you? And as for everything being my fault, if I hadn't come to England, Rosamond would be married to Mr. Denholm by now. For, heaven knows, you would never have lifted a finger to prevent it. And if you had managed to plan your elopement and drive your own equipage, there would have been no need for the captain to become involved. Oh, Rosamond's married the better man all right! Oh, my goodness." She stopped her tirade. "There's no point in our haranguing each other this way."

But she had opened another wound. "The coach!" he said bitterly. "Do you realize they are on their way right now to Scotland in the hackney that *I* paid for?"

Antonia immediately regretted her spontaneous giggle. "What do you mean to do?" she asked solicitously to cover it. "You could perhaps still catch them. Rosamond's not exactly a good traveler, as we can testify."

He gave her a withering look. "I will not demean myself. Rosamond has made her choice. I shall return to Kent. And I pray God that no breath of this scandal shall ever reach my parish. I shall be ruined. Good day, Miss Thorpe."

"Good day?" she echoed. He might as well have said "good riddance." "You feel no responsibility for me, then?"

"My responsibility is to my calling," the man of the cloth replied. "And the fact that I forgot my higher duty and embroiled myself in such a disgraceful coil shall be a thorn in my flesh forever. So, don't ask me to risk sure disgrace by traveling, publicly, in your company, Miss Thorpe. Again, I say good day."

After first opening the door a crack to make sure no one was there, Mr. Hollingsworth eased out into the hall. The door shut softly behind him.

Antonia read Rosamond's letter one more time to assure herself of its reality. She sighed and reached for her reticule. A quick count confirmed what she'd concluded. She had just enough money to pay for her room (for she'd bet a monkey Rosamond hadn't done so) and her coach fare back to London, if she was lucky. But there was no way her meager resources were going to provide for breakfast.

While Antonia had been obliviously asleep, Lady Thirkell and Mrs. Blakeney were up and drinking tea. Lady Thirkell was wearing a brilliant purple dressing gown. Mrs. Blakeney's costume was more subdued but gained a certain dash from the curl papers she was wearing. Mr. Denholm had recently roused their household, then gone storming off, after making sure that Antonia wasn't, after all, safe home in her bed.

"What I do not understand," Mrs. Blakeney spoke peevishly, "is why he has taken it upon himself to go after them that way. I know elopements are not quite the thing, but it is not as though Captain Crosland will not marry her."

"Oh, Captain Crosland has no intention of marrying Antonia. That man's been dangling after a fortune from the very first."

"Oh, dear." Mrs. Blakeney put down her teacup and clutched her heart.

"Quit jumping to conclusions, Claire," Lady Thirkell snapped. "If Thayer saw what he said he saw, the only reason for Antonia to be driving a hackney coach with that captain fellow inside it was that there was another passenger. Crosland's eloped with Rosamond, of course."

"Oh." Mrs. Blakeney tried to cope with conflicting emotions, relief that her granddaughter was not embarked upon a life lived in the shadows, and disappointment that the dashing captain was lost to her forever. "Then, it's Rosamond that Mr. Denholm's chasing after."

"Nothing of the kind! Fitzhugh is pursuing Antonia."

"Don't tell me that *he* intends to offer my granddaughter a carte blanche."

Lady Thirkell sighed. "Really, Claire, your mind does seem to travel a well-worn path. Of course he won't offer Antonia a carte blanche. When he gets around to thinking logically—if a man in love can ever reach that happy state— he'll offer for her. Right now the only thing on his mind

170

is to stop her from eloping with Crosland. For I doubt it will occur to him either that Rosamond's along. And to think I used to consider him the only intelligent member of his generation in the family.''

"Well, I can't say much for *your* intelligence if you think Mr. Denholm will marry Antonia. He's promised to Rosamond and in love with Lady Hastings.''

"In love with that trollop!'' Lady Thirkell snorted her contempt. "Anyone who ever looked at him and not just at that sap-skull in the trollop's play would know he's no longer in love with her. And furthermore, it's my opinion that he never was.''

"Well, Kate''—Mrs. Blakeney, who was beginning to feel a bit more the thing, poured out fresh cups of tea—"you've always been much better at reading human nature than I. But we both know that Worth will never approve.''

"I don't think Worth's approval or disapproval will have anything to say to their marriage. But it will make things much more comfortable all around if he gives them his blessing—which of course he'll do when he learns Antonia's inheriting my fortune.''

Mrs. Blakeney all but dropped her teacup. She managed finally to set it down with shaking hands. "You mean you've actually made Antonia your heir?'' she gasped.

"Well, actually, no. Fitzhugh's that. Thirkell named him when the boy was still at Eton. Never told him, though. Thought it better not to. But there's no reason Worth shouldn't think everything's meant for Antonia. Amounts to the same thing in the end, and it will do marvels in smoothing the gel's way. For there's no use thinking otherwise. The Thirkell fortune will make Sir Edwin Thorpe's seem paltry. That jackanapes!'' She chuckled wickedly.

The only bit of good fortune Antonia had had all day was to secure a seat by the window in the public coach. Not only was she able to contemplate the view, but she was spared a bit of the aroma of the large man next to her, who, besides having an aversion to soap and water, seemed immoderately partial to garlic. She occupied her time by thinking up, and then discarding, various explanations of her complicity for use when her grandmother and Lady Thirkell should learn of Rosamond's rackety elopement. And as for Uncle Edwin (Antonia shuddered, causing her neighbor to ask solicitously if she had a chill), if he did not have her head delivered on a platter, she'd be much surprised.

Traffic on the London Road grew heavy. The coachman made frequent use of his horn to announce their approach as they bore down on a loaded cart or rounded a blind curve. Antonia was glad to trade her morbid thoughts for the distraction of observing and being observed by the passengers in the other carriages who were traveling the way they'd come.

She became even more distracted when their coach's progress grew suddenly erratic. The inside passengers gave one another knowing looks, not untinged with fear. The garlic person expressed aloud what each was thinking: "One of them flash coves up there has took over the reins, or I'm a Dutchman."

Antonia nodded. At the last posting house she, too, had noticed the pair of well-dressed young gentlemen, on holiday from school most likely, who had joined the passengers on top. They must have greased the coachman's palm for the privilege of driving. The blare of the horn grew louder, more frequent. The one not holding the reins was obviously in charge of the "yard of tin."

With her newly developed expertise, Antonia assessed the substitute coachman's skill and found it sadly wanting. "Brace yourselves," she warned her fellow travelers. They were taking the curve much, much too fast. What's more, they were straying well across the highway's center. The horn blared frantically.

Denholm, in his speeding curricle, did his best. He heard the tinny warning and coach wheels coming fast. He took

172

the curve as close to the edge of the highway as safety would allow. All might have yet been well if the young stage driver had not panicked and jerked the reins. The four horses swerved suddenly to their left. As Denholm tooled his team expertly round the careening coach, he heard someone scream his name and glimpsed a familiar, badly frightened face. He tugged and cursed his horses to a halt while he watched with sickening, helpless horror as the stagecoach headed for the ditch, where it rocked back and forth precariously before coming to rest at last on an acute angle against an apple tree. As Antonia was knocking the garlic breath out of the fat man with the impact of her body, Denholm came leaping from his curricle and sprinted toward the wreck. "This has become a habit," he observed as he dragged her up and out. "Are you all right?"

Chapter Twenty

Fitzhugh Denholm reluctantly set Antonia Thorpe upon her feet. He returned to help the other passengers out of the tilted coach and then, by combining manpower with horsepower, succeeded in getting the vehicle back on the road again. Once assured that no real damage had been done to passengers, cattle, or coach, Denholm's intention had been to give the greenhorn driver and irresponsible coachman a good dressing-down, if not actual levelers. But he soon discovered that the angry passengers were sufficient unto themselves in that department. He returned instead to Antonia, who stood a bit apart, obviously still shaken.

"Where's your luggage? Or do you have any?"

"Up there." She pointed to the coach top. "But you mustn't concern yourself with me. I'm sorry I shouted. You should not have stopped. They've got a tremendous head start on you as it is. Go on now. I'll be all right. That idiot won't drive again."

Denholm climbed up, pulled her portmanteau out of the pile of baggage, then took her none too gently by the arm and steered her toward his rig. "Do you know that I haven't the vaguest notion of what you're raving on about? Or why you were in that coach alone? But we can sort it out while I take you home." He more lifted than handed her into the curricle.

"But you mustn't waste time with me," she protested as he climbed aboard and picked up the reins. "Oh, don't turn around, you gudgeon! Scotland's that way."

"I know my geography, Miss Thorpe," he snapped. "But you aren't going to Scotland. Where's your pride, girl? Give it up, I tell you."

"I'd be glad to," she spit back as he sprang his horses in the London direction. "Goodness knows I never wanted to go there in the first place. But I refuse to be blamed when you don't catch up with Rosamond."

He turned to stare. "What the devil does Rosamond have to do with this? No, wait; don't answer. First things first. What the devil have you done with Crosland? I can only hope you came to your senses and left him high and dry. I know how worried you've been about your future, but how you could have even considered running off with that—that—toadeater is beyond understanding. I never thought you lacked for sense, Antonia."

It was her turn to stare. "Are you saying that you think *I* eloped with Captain Crosland? But that's ridiculous. I'd never do such a ramshackle thing. And when it comes to that," she added fairly, "he'd certainly not elope with me. The man's a fortune hunter. What ever gave you such a rackety notion anyhow?"

"Why, Thayer saw you and him together at the Old Bull and Horn. Oh, my God!" Relief was struggling with chagrin. "What an idiot I've been. I went off half-cocked and never took the time to sort things out."

"You mean you came chasing after me?" Her eyes were wide.

"Oh, yes."

"Grandmother sent you, I daresay."

"Not at all. I think she would have been most contented with the match. Aunt Kate, of course, doubted that Crosland would actually marry a penniless girl."

"Oh, I see." Antonia sounded decidedly let down. "It was Lady Thirkell who sent you after me."

"Wrong again. It was my own idea entirely. I only rousted them out of their beds in order to make sure you weren't in yours. Thayer isn't the most reliable of witnesses, you see. Or so I thought. But if my brain had only been working, I'd have stopped to sort out what he said. For he told me he saw you driving a hackney and then saw Crosland climb out of the coach. I should have been able to deduce from that odd displacement that the good captain was keeping someone else company inside. My God, what a fool I've been!" He slapped his forehead. "I should have realized that little miss meddlesome was up to her old tricks, helping her cousin elope with the dashing captain."

"Well, not exactly. But that's close enough."

"Oh, Lord, wrong again. I don't think my self-esteem can bear it. But, go on. Don't spare me. Just what the hell were you up to, Antonia?"

"I was helping Rosamond elope with the Reverend Hollingsworth."

"Rosamond ran off with the curate? I wouldn't have thought either of them had that much enterprise. But then, of course they didn't." He sounded resigned. "That would have been where you came in. But Thayer surely couldn't have mistaken Hollingsworth for Crosland. Not even he could get that confused. I fear to ask—but why was the captain along?"

She sighed. "Must we go into all of this? Yes, I suppose we must," she added quickly, since he looked dangerous. "But, I warn you, you're going to think I've made the whole thing up, for such a pudding-hearted approach to an elopement defies belief even to the average person. And for an old campaigner like yourself who, alone and unabetted, managed to seduce a married woman, fight a duel with her husband, then run away with her to Italy, well, you aren't likely to countenance a word of what I say."

"What I'm likely to do is throttle you if you don't get

176

on with your recital. Only first let me say, ungentlemanly though it may be, that you've got my history right except for one minor point. I was not so much seducer as seducee.''

"Oh."

"But we were discussing Crosland's part in your latest escapade.'' The reins were slack now in his hands, and the horses could have been mere plodders, so snail-like was their pace.

"Well, yes. As you know, Rosamond has never wished to marry you.'' She assessed his expression and hastened on. "So, when Uncle Edwin wrote that you were told to offer for her right away, her first hope was that you yourself would go back to Lady Hastings. But then her ladyship informed Captain Crosland—''

"At last! The captain!''

"Lady Hastings informed Captain Crosland—they've become good friends, you know—that you had told her you intended to marry Rosamond. So she—Rosamond, I mean to say—decided that there was nothing for it but to run off to Gretna Green with the Reverend Hollingsworth.

"Looking back on matters now, I should have known from all the obstacles she threw in our path that Rosamond really did not wish to wed the curate. But then, Rosamond's sense of propriety is so overblown—for instance, her attitude toward your past history always seemed decidedly excessive—oh, for goodness sake, don't fly off into the boughs again. I'll get to the point. Well, as I was saying, when Rosamond refused to go to Gretna Green alone with Mr. Hollingsworth and insisted that I accompany them, it did seem absurd but entirely within character nonetheless.''

"Crosland!'' Denholm said between his teeth.

"I'm coming to him. Heavens, we've miles to go yet. Oh, very well. Arranging an elopement, as it happened, was completely outside the curate's scope. I suppose it

177

isn't the sort of thing they touch on in theological preparation. So Captain Crosland was forced to make all the arrangements: drive the hackney coach, collect Rosamond's baggage—you'd not believe the number of boxes; oh, never mind—work out the route, decide where to change horses, which inns to patronize. And then Rosamond did not wish to hire a coachman for fear he'd gossip about them, and Hollingsworth could not drive.'' She came close to sneering. ''I volunteered to do so myself, but Rosamond would not hear of it. Now, of course, I know the reason why.''

''I can think of several.''

''Well, you'd be mistaken, for as your friend observed, I did drive partway, and most skillfully, if I do say so.'' After this setdown, she seemed to think her narrative was finished.

''Antonia!'' She was jerked from her reverie to find Denholm glaring at her.

''Yes?''

''Are you going to explain why you were on the public coach while the other three, I presume, continued on to Scotland, or must I choke it from you?''

''Oh, that. I thought I'd made it plain. When I woke up this morning, Rosamond was gone. She'd run off with Captain Crosland.''

Denholm stared incredulously. ''You're bamming me! You're not!'' Suddenly he doubled up with laughter. It proved infectious. Antonia joined in.

After they'd subsided, she wiped her eyes. ''I t-told you it was all too absurd. But after I'd got over the shock of the thing I couldn't help but feel it was for the best. Rosamond and Captain Crosland should deal well together. At least, they will if Uncle Edwin doesn't cut them off, which I doubt he'll do, once his anger cools. Oh, I know the captain's a gazetted fortune hunter. But he does have the patience of Job, and I think he really cares for Rosamond. If you could have seen his solicitude when she was getting

178

sick every mile or so and he had to stop the horses." Denholm went off into whoops again, and again she joined him. "And as for Mr. Hollingsworth," she continued once they'd recovered, "I don't care if he is a curate, I've rarely known such an odious man."

"You're saying, then, that Rosamond did well to change horses at the posting house?" He struggled to keep his face straight this time, then succumbed once more. "Well," he was finally able to say, "I hope you've learned a lesson."

"Whatever do you mean?" Antonia bristled. "I had nothing to say to any of this."

"Oh, did you not? It seems to me that you've been busy as a bee of late promoting disastrous matches. And while we're on that subject, do you mind telling me just why you were so eager to fling me at Eugenia's head?"

"I wasn't. What I mean to say is, it was all Captain Crosland's notion that you and Lady Hastings would fall into each other's arms once you were brought together."

"And you wished for that happy conclusion, did you?"

"No. Yes. Oh, everybody was convinced that you really loved her—and only pride stood in your way. So I thought it was the right thing to do. Help you along, I mean. Besides, I know it's not a cousinly admission, but having you married to Lady Hastings would have been easier to bear than having you married to Rosamond."

"I see." He gazed at her thoughtfully. "Everybody was wrong, you know."

"I beg your pardon?"

'The 'everybody' that was convinced I loved Eugenia was all wrong. Our history, I'm afraid, does me no credit." His face reflected the misery he was feeling. "And telling it is ungallant to the point of caddishness. But you have to hear it. Oh, damn it all, Tonia, I was a twenty-year-old

179

green 'un when I met Eugenia. And well, you've seen her.''

"Oh, yes." She sounded as miserable as he looked.

"And, well, she made advances—that I was more than happy to comply with. Often. But the truth was, I was pretty well bored with the whole affair and looking for a gentlemanly—if you'll pardon the use of such a term—way to break it off when her husband caught us, and the rest is history. Or drama, if you like. Of course, I had to take her to Italy with me then. We stayed together for a little while. And I kept on supporting her when she found more entertaining companions. It was a fortuitous escape for both of us when Hastings turned up again and inherited that title. So you see"—his smile was twisted—"it's all a pretty sordid story. I'm a far cry from that romantic hero on stage at Drury Lane.''

"Thank goodness!" The comment was soul-felt. "I thought him insufferable."

"Did you, by God?" He grinned, then quickly sobered. "In fact, what I've most feared I am, Tonia, is inconstant. I've grown to doubt, you see, that I could ever love any woman for very long."

"Yes," she answered thoughtfully, "I can see where you might feel that way, having fallen out of love with such a diamond of the first water."

"But I've given the matter considerable thought since you first started to plague my life."

"What an odious thing to say."

"I know. Hardly romantic, is it? But I don't know how else to describe my state since that morning I walked into your uncle's library and interrupted your letter-writing. I've not been the same man since. You've been full of surprises, Tonia. And, well, I can't bear the thought of not knowing what you'll be up to a month—a year—thirty years from now. I know this is a negative way to put things, but whereas before the thought of having to live a lifetime with one woman seemed intolerable, the thought of not spending

180

the rest of my days with you is totally unacceptable. What I'm trying to say, and making such a mull of, is that I've come to realize there's a world of difference between real love and mooncalf infatuation. Do you think you could marry me, Tonia, warts and all?''

She stared up at him. "Are you offering for me? For *me*?''

"Why all the surprise? It's hardly the first time.''

"But you can't possibly marry me. Your father—''

"Damn my father. If he's too big a fool to realize you're the most wonderful thing that's ever happened to me, he's not worth pleasing. I love you, Tonia. I want you for my wife. For the fourth or fifth time, will you marry me?''

Whatever she might have answered was interrupted by the sound of a rig approaching fast. Another curricle drew up beside them with a young sprig of fashion holding the reins. "Oh, I say, sir . . .''—he gave Denholm an impish grin,—"devilish fine-looking cattle you have there. Appearances can be deceiving, though. Since you're practically limping along, I take it they ain't goers.''

Antonia leaned forward and asked sweetly, "Are you wishing to find out, sir?''

"Antonia!'' Denholm scowled a warning.

The young gentleman's grin widened. He recognized a kindred soul. "Would you care to wager a pound that my pair'll beat yours to a church about a mile and a half from here?''

"Done!'' cried Antonia.

"Now!'' The young man cracked his whip and flew.

"Spring 'em! He's getting away! Do hurry!''

Denholm sat with folded arms. "Not till you say you'll marry me.''

"Of course I'll marry you. But what does that have to say to anything?'' She lunged for the reins, which he managed to keep just out of reach. "Either spring those horses, you widgeon, or let me do it!''

181

"Yes, ma'am." His long whip snaked out with the crack of a dueling pistol just above the horses' ears. They were off like a bullet from that same weapon as Antonia's bonnet went spiraling from her head. Fresh as though they'd just come from the stables, the team of horses galloped down the highway. Antonia began to cheer as the distance rapidly closed between the curricles. When a small white church with an overweening steeple came in sight, Denholm made his move. He sped past the other vehicle while the love of his life gaily waved her handkerchief in a taunting farewell.

The Honorable Fitzhugh Denholm swerved into the churchyard and pulled up his scarcely winded pair. He turned with a grin toward Antonia, who flung herself into his arms, her cheeks flushed with victory, her eyes sparkling. "Oh, that was famous. You really are a nonesuch."

"In all departments," he murmured as his mouth met hers.

So eagerly did she cooperate, so absorbed did they become, that neither noticed the other curricle draw up beside them. The young gentleman cleared his throat politely and, getting no response, watched with interest for a moment, then shrugged and tossed the pound note upon their carriage seat and left.

Much, much later, Denholm reluctantly released his betrothed and stared at her speculatively as she sought to straighten her disarranged garments and smooth her tangled hair. "Tonia, love," his voice mused tenderly, "effective as it is, we really must find another aphrodisiac."

" 'Aphro'—what? I haven't the faintest notion what you're talking about."

"I mean, it's simply not going to be practical to get out my rig, harness my team, and find some young fool to race us neck-or-nothing every time I wish to make love to you."

"You really are absurd." Her face was scarlet nonethe-

182

less as they circled the little church and returned to the London highway.

On the outskirts of the city they stopped again to watch a glorious sunset that boded fair. When the last streaks of red were dimming in the sky and the lamps of London began to twinkle in the distance, Antonia, who for some time had been quite thoughtful, now observed, "It's odd, isn't it, how people's characters and their lives can be so contradictory. Take Grandmama, for instance. Her life has been a scandal. Yet no one's more anxious for propriety than she is. And now here you are—a notorious rake—bent on becoming a veritable pattern card of virtue."

"Disappointed?"

"Not in the least." The smile she flashed him caused his pulse to race. "But it does make one wonder what the gossipmongers will find to chew on now while they sip their scandal broth."

"Well, there's always your Cousin Rosamond."

"Oh, yes, Rosamond." She chuckled. "Now there's a case in point. No one—with the possible exception of Uncle Edwin—has ever been more concerned with doing the proper than my cousin. And how does she, in the final analysis, live up to her principles? By eloping with two fiancés at once! My heavens, that almost rivals your own Lady Eugenia Lytton Hastings! I think I'll write a play about it."

"You do and I'll throttle you. No, cancel that threat. I'm not worried about you in the least, my love. For I have a foolproof scheme to keep you out of mischief." He flicked his reins and guided his horses off the verge where they'd been standing. Once firmly on the high road, he cracked his whip and urged the team to an incredible burst of speed.

"What on earth do you think you're doing?" Antonia clutched his sleeve to keep from sliding off the leather as they went flying round a curve.

183

"Looking for another curricle to race!" he shouted, and grinned lasciviously. "There's bound to be one on up ahead there somewhere. I can hardly wait!"

The whip cracked again as the smart sporting rig went tooling on toward London and toward a future that, like the fading sunset, boded fair.

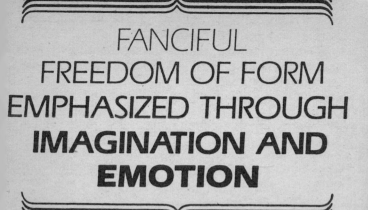

FANCIFUL
FREEDOM OF FORM
EMPHASIZED THROUGH
IMAGINATION AND
EMOTION

Marion Devon

By the year 2000, 2 out of 3 Americans could be illiterate.

It's true.

Today, 75 million adults...about one American in three, can't read adequately. And by the year 2000, U.S. News & World Report envisions an America with a literacy rate of only 30%.

Before that America comes to be, you can stop it...by joining the fight against illiteracy today.

Call the Coalition for Literacy at toll-free **1-800-228-8813** and volunteer.

**Volunteer
Against Illiteracy.
The only degree you need
is a degree of caring.**

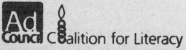

Ad Council   Coalition for Literacy

LV-2